BLOOD CURSE

by

William Blackwell

Acknowledgements

Heartfelt thanks to my loyal and supportive friends and family, the hardworking staff at Telemachus Press, and my editor. Special thanks to the Government of Prince Edward Island for its financial support.

Blood Curse

Cover designed by Telemachus Press LLC

Published by Telemachus Press LLC

Paperback ISBN: 978-1-0697318-5-2

Version: 2016.12.01

The boundaries which divide Life from Death are at best shadowy and vague. Who shall say where the one ends, and where the other begins?

—Edgar Allan Poe

PROLOGUE

It had been four years. Sure there were good years, but they were in the beginning. Year one was probably the best. After that things started to slide. Year two had its moments, but that's the year Mac noticed Livia Johnson's attentions starting to wander. She would stare a little too long at a handsome man, a pedestrian on the street perhaps. In restaurants, she would flirt with handsome waiters—a little too long for what might be considered healthy flirtation. At first Mac didn't mind. *Let them ogle her. I'm the one taking her home to bed. She can work out all that sexual frustration on me.* But after a while, the flirtations became a little bolder, as if Livia was testing how far she could go before Mac blew up. Initially, he had kept his mouth shut. But the game was wearing thin. And, more than that, it was becoming painful. He had started with small comments, delivered evenly and without anger.

"Do you have to ogle him so long? I thought that smile was reserved for me? You kissed him? On the lips? I know it's a party but you hardly know him. You shouldn't let him touch you like that. Those areas are reserved for me."

But Livia always had an answer, accompanied by that infectious smile and seductive wink.

"Don't be so insecure. It's just harmless fun... Sure he's good-looking but you're my man... It was just an innocent kiss... We're just good friends, that's all... He didn't touch my boob. It was my shoulder. If I wasn't going out with you, I'd want a man just like him. But I am going out with you. You're my man forever."

It was building up inside Mac and reaching a boiling point. He just hoped he could control his explosive temper. It had gotten the better of him in the past, resulting in a litany of profanity and saying things he later regretted. He hoped three years of psychotherapy had fixed that.

At least his shrink had said, "You've come a long way, Mac. You're not the same person you once were."

He hoped that was true.

Yesterday, early evening, Mac and Livia had arrived at Vancouver's Locarno Beach for the weekly scratch volleyball game. A mid-summer night's game. It was a non-competitive, friendly affair that usually included plenty of alcohol during and after. Things had started well. Twelve people had arrived. They picked teams of five, with two participants standing out doing rotation. It also gave them an opportunity to swill some beer on the sidelines while waiting their turn to take the sand court.

Livia had stepped out along with a new arrival, a tall muscular man with a shock of black hair, a carefree attitude, and a winning smile. Lance was his name. They stood on the sidelines while the others played. Mac tried to concentrate on the game but couldn't help overhearing Lance and Livia's conversation.

Livia: "Did anyone ever tell you, you look like Johnny Depp?"

Lance chuckled and ogled her fine cleavage. "Yeah, I've heard it quite a bit actually."

"You do. You're gorgeous."

Lance moved closer to her ample bosom. "Thanks, you're pretty hot yourself."

Livia blushed, brushing back a lock of her long red hair. "It's Lance, right?"

"That's right." He'd moved closer, extending a hand. "Nice to meet you, Livia."

Mac stopped and stared. A spike serve smashed off his head followed by uproarious laughter.

"Pay attention," Joe Samson, his competitive friend said. "We're losing. Set me up for a spike on the next one."

Mac nodded. "Sorry. Will do."

While an opposing team member prepared to serve, Mac glanced at the sidelines again. The greeting that had started off as a handshake had turned into a hug. And a kiss. On the lips.

He felt a hot flush crawl across his face, his blood boil with rage. It was all he could do to control it. "Joe," he said, "you set me, I'll come in from behind."

Joe grinned and gave him the thumbs up.

"We'll be right back," Livia said, walking arm-in-arm with Lance across the sand toward the parking lot. "I'm going to help Lance with his cooler."

Mac frowned.

The ball was served to the back court. It was bumped up high and Joe, playing net, moved under it.

"You ready?"

"Go for it."

Joe volleyed a perfect set about four feet from the net, a high floater. Mac moved in and hammered the ball hard. It smashed into the face of Laura Whitehorn, almost knocking her off her feet. She staggered, put her hands to her face, knelt down and started crying. When she looked up, a red volleyball imprint was tracking up her face and along her forehead.

"Hey," a tall beefy player shouted, "this is supposed to be a friendly game. Not so fucking hard, man."

"Sorry," Mac said, approaching Laura. "You okay? I didn't mean that. I'll tone it down."

Laura wiped away tears, looking at him with narrowing eyes.

"You think this is the fucking Olympics or something?" the beefy player said. "We're here to have fun. You wanna play competitive like that, get your male buds together and don't invite me."

"Sorry," Mac said. "It won't happen again."

Laura was escorted to the sidelines and after a beer-break the game resumed.

Livia had not returned with Lance. Mac was about to go check on her. He had noticed them disappear inside a black van. Suddenly, he saw her step out, sipping a vodka cooler. She tucked a white piece of paper into her tight blue jean shorts that left little to the imagination.

Out of the corner of his eye, he watched them return. Lance also carried a cooler. They talked and laughed amicably. Livia was beaming.

Mac bit his tongue and controlled the rage. He drove Livia home after the game, gave her a peck on the cheek, and drove home.

There was a time and a place for everything, his shrink had taught him.

******

Now, he thought, as he laid in bed in Livia's apartment early the following evening. *Now's the time. Now's the place.*

She was in the bathroom freshening up, getting ready to go out for dinner with Mac. Or so she thought. They had just had sex. Mac hadn't planned the sex part. But those tight pink shorts, the white t-shirt barely concealing voluptuous, braless, breasts, had created a little diversion to the plan. Besides he hadn't had sex in over two weeks; sometimes Livia just wasn't in the mood. So they had had okay sex, definitely devoid of passion, at least on Mac's part. Livia seemed to enjoy it, lying there moaning, but doing little else in the way of foreplay or fondling.

Earlier that day, Mac had packed up the few belongings she had kept at his apartment—pink lace panties, a few shirts, two pairs of shorts, a toiletry bag with women's things, and a toothbrush—and had put them in his vehicle. He had also brought his knapsack which he had planned on using to pack up the few items he had at Livia's. He got up. *Now's the time. Now's the place.*

He dressed quickly and began throwing assorted articles of his clothing in the knapsack. He finished. He still had a toothbrush in her bathroom, but fuck it. She could keep it.

He flung the knapsack over his shoulder. "I'll be back in a minute. I left my smokes in the car."

From the bathroom, "Okay sweetie."

He put the knapsack into his car and grabbed two plastic grocery bags containing her things. He entered the apartment, set them down on her kitchen table, and went into the bedroom.

She was still prettying herself up in the bathroom.

On an impulse, he opened the top drawer of the mirrored vanity and reached inside. He had seen her put papers in there before. He pulled out five or six pieces of paper, men's names and phone numbers scrawled on them. Lance's was there. He stifled an urge to break down and cry and another to smash a fist into the mirror. Whether he wanted to admit it to himself or not, he had fallen in love with Livia. This wasn't going to be easy.

He waited for the emotions to pass. They didn't entirely. *Never do things out of anger or jealously*, his shrink had warned him. It was too late.

"Livia?"

"What honey?"

"Could you come out here for a second?"

"I'll just be a minute."

THIS CAN'T WAIT A FUCKING MINUTE, YOU CHEATING BITCH! he thought.

"I don't think this can wait," he said.

Carrying a blow dryer, she entered the bedroom, a white towel draped around her body. Her hair was frizzed up afro-style all around her head, as if she had stuck her finger in an electrical outlet.

Frowning, Mac raised a handful of pieces of paper.

"What are you doing going through my things?" she said. "Can't a woman have any privacy?"

"I opened one drawer and found these," Mac said evenly, his face beginning to flush. He threw them into the air and they drifted to the floor like confetti. "Listen, if you think I can do a relationship like this, you're dead wrong girl. I saw the way you flirted with Lance. I see now you have his number..."

"Can't a girl have friends?" Livia said, stepping forward.

Mac stepped back. "Don't. Don't come near me."

She stopped. "Mac, this is nothing, I promise. I love you. I would never sleep with any of those men. I was just making friends—that's all. What's wrong with that? You have woman friends. I don't get jealous."

"You think that's okay what you're doing? You think you can ogle all those men, collect their phone numbers, probably fuck them for all I know, and that's okay? I've had my women friends for a long time. I'm not out soliciting relationships. How do you think that makes me feel, seeing you act like that in public?"

Livia sat on the bed, put down the blow dryer and wiped a hand over wet eyes. She looked at him pleadingly. "They're just friends. I promise. I never planned on doing anything with them. Maybe I just like the attention, which you don't always give me."

"And why do you think I don't always give it to you, Livia? Why? Because you act like a two-bit tramp that's why."

She raised a hand in a supplicating gesture, offering hurt little brown eyes. "Sit down and let's talk about this."

The towel had slipped down, revealing most of a large white breast and half of a large pink areola.

"I'm sorry, Livia. There's nothing more to talk about. Your shit from my apartment is on your kitchen table."

Now the tears started to stream down her face. "No, Mac, please."

He approached the bedroom door. "It's over."

She stood, adjusting the towel and approached. Mac was already out of the bedroom, reaching the main door.

She followed.

As he opened the door, she grabbed his shoulder. He shrugged her off, turned and faced her. They locked eyes. A black shadow crossed her hurt expression and her eyes flared red. "You'll get yours. Karma's a bitch. You want to treat women like this, you'll get yours."

Mac stepped outside and turned to face her. "Why don't you tell that to someone who cares. I don't ever want to see you again. Lose my fucking phone number. Hell, you've got plenty of others anyway. Maybe Lance will want to listen to your bullshit."

She was yelling now, shaking her fists as Mac hurried to his vehicle. "YOU'RE A FUCKING ASSHOLE AND I WILL SEE YOU GET YOUR COMEUPPANCE!!"

Mac couldn't resist the urge. He rolled down the window, flipped the double-bird, said "Fuck you... you fucking bitch," and drove away, the clacking engine of his diesel pick-up drowning out her yelling retort.

Chapter One

He didn't even know her name.

It had been, what, three weeks now, of stopping by the Petro Canada service station in small-town Montague, PEI, just to see her and he still didn't even know her name. And it wasn't for lack of reminding himself. As he pulled into the parking lot, or pulled up to the gas pump, Mackenzie Adamson would tell himself, *Check for a nametag... they all have nametags.*

But once he entered the store and took one look at her, he would forget. He didn't know why he forgot, but Mac had his theories. The way she looked at him. Those soulful brown eyes; that cute little dimple on her right cheek, the easy way she smiled, the innocent way she would dart her eyes away from him if they stayed a little longer than what was considered polite. And her hair. He loved her long natural blonde hair and the disarming way she brushed away a lock that seemed to have a mind of its own and would dangle loose and sweep across her sight-line while she leaned to ring something through the cash register.

Then there was the other theory, which heretofore Mac had been unwilling to fully espouse, either privately to himself or publicly to one of his friends. *What friends?* Why? Because it involved his feelings, feelings that he had a hard time believing were real. What were the feelings, or feeling? Love at first sight. Mac thought the notion was as silly as putting ketchup in chicken noodle soup, although he knew people did it.

But, why, he asked himself as he wheeled his trusty Dodge pick-up into a customer parking stall at *the* service station, did he always feel so euphoric and light-headed after seeing the Petro Canada chick—*get her name this time, you idiot*—with her radiant smile, or engaging in some light-hearted small-talk about something as mundane as the weather? *You like her admit it. You love her. Don't be daft.*

He turned the wipers and the ignition off and stared outside at the black sky and the snowflakes already gathering on the windshield. It was only five-thirty-six in the afternoon but it felt like ten-thirty at night. In December the night snatched away the day early. Outside it was a frigid minus-nine degrees Celsius but, with the wind-chill, it felt like minus-nineteen. The weather man had predicted winds in access of 100 kilometers an hour and another ten to fifteen centimeters of snow by midnight tonight.

A nasty Atlantic storm was on its way.

Mac glanced in the mirror at his two-day stubble and scraped a hand over its sandpapery surface. He smiled for the mirror and then frowned, thinking it came off as forced, unnatural, not anything like *her* smile. He pulled his black Budweiser baseball cap down so the wind wouldn't sweep it off his head and put on his black cotton gloves.

He wasn't self-conscious about his lack of fashion sense regarding the baseball cap. At least in the rural areas, many men wore them, even some women. You fit in like a glove in cold weather here. Even in Charlottetown, the big city with a whopping forty-odd thousand people, locals didn't look at you askance if you were wearing a baseball cap—even in the banks, restaurants and a lot of bars. The baseball cap here was to the male population what a flashy suit might be to a stock broker on Wall Street. It almost made you fit in.

Almost, but in Mac's case, not quite.

The weather, he thought, as a gust of cold wind chilled him to the bone as soon as he stepped out of the truck. He shivered. *That'll be an easy one. Talk about the upcoming storm, the expected power outages, blah, blah.*

Mac sighed deeply. He wanted more than just small-talk about the weather. For three weeks he had made any excuse whenever he left his rural oceanfront acreage on Blackberry Grove, a short twenty-minute drive to Montague, to stop at Petro Canada and see her. Before he left, whether he planned on approaching her or not, he would dutifully remind himself to put a business card and a pen in his top shirt pocket to make it easy to swap numbers. When it didn't make sense to fill up with gas, he would buy gum, cigarettes, coffee, chocolate, whatever, just as an excuse to make contact. He wanted to be friends with this woman. He wanted to date her. He wanted her as his girlfriend. He wanted her to move in with him. He wanted to marry her. And he thought that was the only thing that could save him from the isolation, loneliness and despair he was starting to feel since relocating here from the big city.

Opening the door, he touched the top pocket. Good. The business card and the pen were there. And looking up, he realized, so was she. There were two tills, two cashiers, and a line of customers. In between ringing a customer purchase through, she acknowledged him with that infectious smile. "Hi, how are you?"

"Good."

For the first time in three weeks, he remembered. He looked at her chest and there it was, just like he had imagined: a plastic white nametag marked with Ophelia in black letters. *She doesn't look like an Ophelia. Never mind. It's a nice name. You're making progress.*

He slipped down an aisle ostensibly to decide on his purchase. He knew what he wanted, a coffee, but he also wanted to browse the candy aisle, kill time so the line-up would thin and it wouldn't be so embarrassing to make conversation with her. With Ophelia. Gazing but not seeing candy bars and gum on display, he extracted the business card, wanting to make sure it was the right one. Sure enough, it was: *Mackenzie Adamson, Editor, SEO Copywriter*. There was also an e-mail address, website, fax, office number, even a twitter handle. No cell number, though, but Mac had solved that problem by writing his cell number on the back. He slid the card into his pocket.

Glancing occasionally at the thinning line, he rehearsed his plan. *So fucking hard*. How do you ask a woman on a date in a busy gas station with another employee standing right beside her, customers coming and going, without coming across as a total fool? Or worse still, a stalker. Mac had been oh-so-close a few times but had chickened out, mainly because of customers and the presence of another female cashier who seemed intent on budding into the conversation. But this time would be different, he had told himself while leaving home to run errands in town about an hour earlier. This time had to be different. He was starting to lose hope. Yes, it was now or never. He had to be confident. He had to forget about that stupid mirror of social judgment and make his move. He had even rehearsed the conversation in his mind.

After the perfunctory small talk:

Mac: "I'm Mac, by the way. I'm new to the Island."

Ophelia, ringing though the purchase, brushing that unruly lock of hair aside: "Ophelia, a pleasure. I kind of gathered that."

Mac: "I don't have a lot of friends here and... well... it would be great if we could get together for a coffee or something, sometime. You know, just as friends."

Ophelia, the smile widening: "I'd like that."

Matt, producing the business card and handing it to her: "Listen, here's my card, I'd really like it if you called me soon. We could make a plan and go out."

Ophelia, reaching for the card cheerily: "I'll definitely call you. I'd love to go out. Have a great day now."

And that would be that—the beginning of a joyful and companioned life. Isolation and loneliness, those dark devils that gnaw on your happiness and sanity, be gone forever, banished to that deleterious abyss from whence you spawned your poisonous, puss-filled fangs.

Mac glanced at the line. Now there was only one customer, a middle-aged woman at Ophelia's till. The other cashier's till was empty and she eyed Mac cheerfully. "Anything I can help you with?"

Mac felt a hot blush crawl across his cheeks. He realized he had been loitering in the candy aisle for too long. Nervously, he returned the smile. "No, just trying to decide."

He approached the coffee counter, poured himself a large medium-roast Columbian, added a squirt of milk, a pinch of sugar, stirred it and glanced at the cashier. Good. The middle-aged woman had finished with her purchase and was heading out the door. He watched her leave, noticing two more cars pull in. His small window of opportunity would slam shut at any second and crush his fragile ego. *Now or never. Make your move.*

He approached Ophelia's cash register.

She brushed away the unruly lock of hair as it danced across her face. She smiled. "How are you today? Haven't seen you here in a while."

Her colleague, a plump pleasant-looking brunette, watched and listened.

Mac had deliberately skipped the last three days out of fear of being labelled a stalker. It was such a politically correct society nowadays one had to be very careful how they conducted themselves. Was this just normal customer friendliness or did Ophelia actually like him? It was impossible to tell, at least for Mac. "I'm good, just been battening down the hatches for the storm is all."

"I hear you. Just the coffee?"

Mac nodded.

She punched number buttons on the cash register. "I hear it's going to get ugly tonight. You know the storm last week my power was out for three hours."

Mac saw a dollar and forty-six cents come up on the digital screen and handed Ophelia a toonie. She started making change. "But I heard it was a lot worse for some others. In Beach Point their power was out for over eight hours."

Change the subject. Get to the point. Your window is closing. But, once started, the polite thing to do was to finish a conversation. "Mine was down for a couple of hours. Even when it went on it was intermittent, kept going out. Every time I'd reset my four digital clocks, about an hour later, I'd have to do it all over again."

Ophelia smiled and handed over change. Briefly, Mac felt the soothing warmth of her touch as her fingers ever so slightly caressed his palm. In contrast to the chilly weather, a comforting warmth shot up his arm. *Did she do that on purpose?*

"Welcome to the Island," she said. "Should have just left them off 'til the wind died down."

"Yeah. I'll know better next time."

"All I did was curl up on the couch beside the woodstove with a blanket and a good book," Ophelia said.

A male customer entered the store, greeted the cashiers with a wave, and went to the pop coolers.

Now, tell her you're new to the Island. Do your spiel. "That's a good idea. I guess you know I'm—"

"What're you reading?" the other cashier, whose nametag said Irma, asked Ophelia.

"Stephen King's *The Stand*. They say it's the bible of post-apocalyptic fiction."

"I love Stephen King," Irma said.

"A great writer," Mac said. "And a great book."

"Oh... you like Stephen King, too?" Ophelia asked.

"Always have." Mac felt deflated but tried hard to hide it. "I love horror and he's one of the masters."

Another female customer entered. It was starting to get real uncomfortable for Mac. She approached Irma's till and handed over a credit card for a gas purchase. The woman looked at Mac like he was a Martian and said, "It's getting real cold out there. I wish I could go south to a beach. But I can't afford it."

By this time, the male customer was standing behind Mac with a bottle of Coca-Cola in his hand and a look of mild annoyance on his face.

"Sorry, I'm distracting you," said Ophelia.

"You can distract me anytime," Mac said, thinking immediately how stupid it sounded—like a cheap come-on line.

But Ophelia smiled. "Have a great day."

"You too."

Inside his truck, the first emotion he felt was anger. He pounded his fist hard on the dashboard.

"Fuck, fuck, fuck and fuck sakes. How the hell am I ever going to be able to ask her out in there? That's damn near impossible."

A few minutes later, driving home on the deserted dimly lit highway, his pick-up was battered by fierce winds and waves of blowing snow. Mac's anger dissipated and was replaced by a mixture of perhaps more debilitating emotions; loneliness first, which gave way to a painful sadness that felt like a rock in the pit of his stomach. Then slowly the sadness gave way to the dark and debilitating hammer of depression. During the drive it had crept up on him, like a small mallet tapping tiny black nails into his head. But now, five minutes from home, the mallet had changed into a sledgehammer and the tiny black nails were giant spikes of doom and gloom, driving out happiness and hope, driving in the debilitating blackness of depression.

Mac hated that word: depression. Just hearing or reading it had the power to make him feel it. And now, pulling into the lonely driveway of his lonely and isolated home on twenty acres, he would have to face it. Alone, and not by himself, as he once prided himself in saying. It wasn't so long ago he had told his Vancouver friend Danny DeLong, three months after relocating to the Island, "I don't like the word alone. I live here by myself. Not alone. Alone has negative connotations. It suggests I'm not happy with my own company. Nothing could be further from the truth."

Pulling the Dodge into the chain-sawed opening of a barn he had recently converted into a garage, he wondered if he still believed his pearls of introspective wisdom. Maybe he believed them, but did they still apply to his current situation?

He exited the truck, turned the barn light on and walked around to the passenger side to retrieve his groceries; three Swanson TV dinners, two frozen pizzas, a loaf of white Wonder bread (shelf-life one year) a quart of two per cent skim milk, eggs, coffee, cereal, bananas, a pack of chocolate-chip cookies, a deli-prepared, pre-cooked chicken dinner, two bags of no-name chips, smokes and a twelve-pack of beer. *Gotta have the staples*.

He opened the door, stared at the bags for a moment, and then decided to hell with it. The groceries could wait. He left the passenger door ajar, returned to the driver side, pulled out his cigarettes and lighter from a side-door compartment, lit one, inhaled deeply and stared out at the black night. Not a star in the sky. Even the moon was covered by the snow-producing clouds. The wind hissed and howled, whipping falling snow into drifts. The tree-tops bordering the house swayed and whistled with the intensity of the coming storm.

Smoking, Mac watched, listened, and felt the impending storm, the old heatless barn offering a modicum of protection from the bone-chilling wind. And he thought about his current situation, trying to reason his way out of the black cloud of depression that was beginning to get a foothold. Just over three months ago, at the age of 45, he had left his job and life in Vancouver on the west coast of Canada and relocated to the turn-of-the-century two-storey home on the east coast of Canada. The job wasn't a big deal; he had worked for the last ten years as a porter at UBC Hospital, taking crazy people to the psych ward, injured and sometimes raving suicidal people to the operating room and Emergency ward, blood samples to the lab, drugs to just about every ward and dead people to the morgue. He had grown tired of it and needed a change. So when Marque Publishing, a Florida-based company, offered him a job as a novel editor working out of the comfort of his own home, he decided why not? Editing done well was an art. What better place to hone his craft than his beautiful if modest home in an inspirational setting in the country? Get out of grid-lock traffic, escape big-city stress, turn a new page, write a new chapter, follow your passion, chase your dreams. It seemed like the perfect opportunity.

So he had sold his downtown condo, packed his bags, left at least a dozen close friends behind and now here he was, "living the dream," as he had told his friends at a surprise going-away party.

But what he hadn't anticipated was the isolation. The loneliness. The deafening sound of the silence. Upon first arriving, August 14, 2013, things had been a lot different. A lot happier, like a honeymoon but without the ball and chain.

He had been in the throes of renovating the house and outbuildings, personalizing his home. It was summer, the weather was hot and sunny, the wildlife; coyotes, eagles, rabbits, squirrels, chipmunks, exciting and amusing. His fourteen-hundred feet of beachfront was a dream come true. Seals and ducks even made their home there. Surely his friends would give their eye-teeth for a place like that. And to be sure, many of them were envious, some perhaps even a little jealous.

He flicked his cigarette ash on the barn's red dirt floor, zipped up his jacket and surveyed the blackness surrounding him. If it was a honeymoon, the honeymoon was over. The renovations were done, the property fixed up to a cozy and habitable condition, and Old Man Winter had invaded, bringing frequent storms, frigid temperatures and lots of snow. Perhaps a typical Canadian winter, but nothing like Vancouver, the most temperate climate in Canada, where instead of snow, oftentimes it rained in the winter and the temperatures rarely dipped below zero degrees Celsius.

Maybe it was an accumulation of rejection that was playing on him. That accumulation that finally on this day had settled into him in the form of depression. A month ago, renovations complete, Mac had made an effort to meet people. Even though he liked the saying, the more people I meet, the more I like my cat, he knew that to survive, thrive and be happy here he needed to establish a close social network, to feel a part of the community. But PEI wasn't exactly a thriving metropolis. The distances, the icy hand of Old Man Winter, made it difficult. Charlottetown, a pretty and historic city, was a fifty-minute commute for Mac. So, in the winter, its distance often ruled it out as a socializing destination. Murray River, a ten-minute drive and the closest town to Mac was, without going into a lot of detail, a one-horse town at best. It didn't even have a pub. So, the next best choice was nearby Montague, a small town with a little more than 6,000 inhabitants, a few bars and plenty of amenities. That's where Mac was concentrating his efforts on making friends and finding a significant other.

His seven-year marriage to pharmacist Melanie Baker—the significant other before Livia—had eroded to the point of divorce four and a half years ago and since then there had been only Livia—that lying, cheating bitch.

But now, Mac felt he was over being livid with Livia, over Melanie.

With Melanie, the relationship hadn't been as tumultuous as it had with Livia. They had split because Melanie had changed her mind. They started by agreeing they didn't want to have children. Five years into the relationship, Melanie decided she wanted two children. Mac didn't.

His mind wandered back to the rejection he was feeling on the Island, the source of most of his loneliness, he believed. He had met an Islander, the word locals use to describe people born on the Island as opposed to those who "come from away," in McNally's Pub one night. Over drinks, Mac and Delbert Mackinnes had exchanged phone numbers.

"I'm new to the Island. I need more friends," Mac had told him. "Maybe we can get together for a beer sometime."

Delbert: "You won't call. You're drunk. Everyone says that, but they don't call."

Mac: "I'll call. Trust me."

And a few days later, Mac did. It went to voice-mail. Mac left a message. No response. He tried a text message. Same story. Another call. More of the same. Rejection. Over time, he was able to right that one in his mind somewhat. Delbert had given him some details of his past, and they weren't exactly of the upwardly mobile sort. He told a story about a woman who had approached him one day in the same bar, saying, "We're kindred spirits, tell me a little about yourself."

To which Delbert responded: "I've had two impaired driving convictions in the last three years, I work for a landscaping company in the summer, collect employment insurance in the winter, and I live with my Mom. I drink every weekend."

The woman's response, before storming away: "You're an alcoholic and a loser."

No, Mac didn't need any social zeroes in his life. But there had been other rejections. In the same bar, one night Mac met an outspoken and amiable man from Texas called Tyrone. A few drinks. A few laughs. The exchange of phone numbers.

Tyrone, taking Mac's card, "That would be awesome. I'll have you over to my place for drinks. I'm sure you like steak, right? I can cook a mean steak. Come over for a barbeque."

A few days later, a few calls. A few texts. No response. More rejection.

Another similar story occurred at a community hall dance in Montague. Out on the deck taking a smoke break, Mac met an Islander by the name of Eddy Berkowitch, who said he was looking for drinking buddies and a competent wing man. Mac volunteered for the job. Eddy accepted. Two days went by, two texts and two phone calls went unanswered.

I'm from fucking away. The hidden meaning—'You're not fucking welcome here.' So many fucking flakes in the world. Don't judge. What, don't judge? That's stupid logic if I ever heard it. If I didn't judge people, I'd end up hanging around with all kinds of derelicts, losers and users. Fuck that, I want to be able to choose my friends carefully.

Mac couldn't help noticing that on the surface Islanders were friendly, but this friendliness in many cases was just that—paper friendliness. It was quite another thing to find your way into their social circles. Many were cliquey. Not anything like Vancouver, where Mac found it easy to make friends. People would welcome you into their hearts and homes, much like Calgary, where he had lived for ten years before moving to Vancouver.

But PEI was different. Islanders were just, well, different.

But the biggest nail—no, spike—in the coffin of despair was the grim realization that it would be next to impossible to land Ophelia, even if his gut feeling was right and she did like him. Women were so hard to read. For all he knew, she was just being friendly. What was he supposed to do, follow her home one day (he had already identified her vehicle, one 1998 yellow Dodge Neon, and recorded its license plate number), step out of his truck and say, "Oh hi Ophelia. We've talked many times at the gas station. I know I'm in your driveway but I was just in the neighborhood and thought I'd stop by. I'm not stalking you, honestly. I'm just, well, desperate for companionship really and I thought maybe we could go for a coffee or something like that. I... I like you. What do you think? How do you like me so far?"

Sure, he thought, crushing out the smoke. *That'll go over like a fucking lead balloon.* He grabbed the grocery bags, flicked the barn light off and, blasted by freezing winds and blowing snow, trudged through the snow and into the house. *I fucking hate the cold.* Putting the groceries away, he realized he was supposed to be thinking his way out of—here comes that word again—depression. But, instead, he was creating more of a funk, widening the black holes left by the spikes of doom and gloom.

Chapter Two

Three hours later, it wasn't all doom and gloom. Using leftovers, Mac had fashioned dinner—scrambled eggs cooked with sliced onions, sliced wieners and toast topped with cheese spread. Unable to think himself out of the funk, he had tried to work himself out of it. For two hours, he had been somewhat successful, doing edits on website copy for a woman in the Dominican Republic who called herself a Voodoo witch, casting spells designed to improve a person's life in finance, love and relationships, health, well-being and inner peace and tranquility. Mac's main source of income was editing manuscripts from new indie authors sent to him from Marque Publishing. But the agreement he had with Marque also allowed him to hang up his own shingle (or website as it were) in which he offered editing and writing services for a wide range of clients.

The request from Voodoo witch Magdeline Ortega had arrived via e-mail a week ago and at first Mac had been reluctant to take the assignment. Like Hollywood movies had portrayed it, he had always viewed Voodoo in a negative light, associated with witches pushing pins into dolls and causing all manner of horrors to spell victims. But Magdeline, or Maggie as she preferred to be called, who resided in Puerto Plata, Dominican Republic, assured Mac over the phone that her Voodoo spells were only for the betterment of her customers and to help them realize their true aspirations in life. She was, she insisted, "a real spell caster and a fourth generation Voodoo witch whose roots began in Haiti." After a ten-minute conversation—man, did she have a smooth and sexy voice—Mac agreed to help her. He had even agreed to her request for a ten per cent discount after she had offered Mac a free Voodoo spell, one that would "solve all your problems, help you with your love interest, and show you the path to happiness, inner peace and tranquility."

Finishing the last of the night's edits at 8:36 pm, he saved the document, closed it and wiped his tired eyes. He doubted he would take Maggie up on the free spell offer but after today's let-down with Ophelia, he hadn't completely ruled it out. He was at his wit's end trying to figure out how to land a date with her. Maybe he needed a powerful Voodoo spell to give him that added edge. His own resources were letting him down and the isolation of country living and the lack of people-contact was starting to give him cabin fever.

As the Doors played, Mac stared out his bay window into blackness, listening to the lyrics, punctuated by one-hundred-kilometer-per-hour wind gusts battering the northern front exposure of his house. Trees swayed, whistled and whipped.

You know the day destroys the night
Night divides the day
Tried to run
Tried to hide
Break on through to the other side
Break on through to the other side
Break on through to the other side, yeah

Remembering he had left some plastic lawn chairs and a table exposed in the back yard, he got up, sure that the furniture would be plastered against the surrounding tree-line, probably splintered into a million pieces by the ferocious winds.

Then his cell phone rang. At first he was going to ignore the call—he wasn't exactly in the headspace for conversation—but then he realized it was his long-time friend Dianna Wilson, a deeply spiritual woman who often propped him up when he was feeling down. Living in Vancouver, she was the type of friend who would drop everything in a heartbeat, jump on a plane, and rush to his aid if he needed her help. A person was lucky if they could count friends like that on one hand. Mac could count them on two.

He answered. After the perfunctory social niceties, she got to the point. Mac knew it wouldn't take long. Dianna wasn't big on mincing words.

"How are you adjusting to Island life?"

"Let's call it a love-hate relationship. It has its good and bad points. I love the property, love the peacefulness and love nature. But I think when I moved here there was something I overlooked."

"What's that?"

"In Vancouver, I just took it for granted that my friends were all around me. You know I like my alone... ah, by myself time. But there, whenever I wanted to see someone, have a drink, coffee, whatever, it was just a phone call away. I miss that."

"I knew you would. You have to understand something, Mac. What you did was an extremely courageous thing. How many people do you know would up and leave their friends all by themselves and start a new chapter alone in a different culture, on an isolated acreage? I know how you're feeling. I've tried it myself and it didn't work."

"It's harder by myself. If I had a partner it would be a lot easier."

"Yes. Then at least you'd have someone to fight with."

Mac forced a chuckle. "Yeah, some drama would be good."

"Exactly. But all by yourself. That's hard. Very hard. Do you have any friends yet?"

"Not really. I made some contacts but they didn't even return my calls."

"Don't take that as rejection. Most of the time you're not in it. It's their own shit."

"Maybe you're right. I do have one friend, though."

"Who?"

Robbie the rabbit. He visits sometimes, but doesn't grace me with his company for long."

"A rabbit. That sounds dismal. You can't talk to a rabbit."

"I talk to Robbie all the time. The more people I meet the more I like my rabbit."

"Have you tried any of the pubs or volunteering, anything like that?"

"Charlottetown is too far for me to hang out. I've been hanging around a pub in Montague a bit. People are friendly, but... it hasn't gone that well. The people here are a little different... cliquey."

"What about women? Any prospects?"

Mac thought he'd save Dianna the Ophelia story.

"No."

"Why don't you go online?"

"Not my thing."

"Maybe you should keep an apartment in Vancouver as well. That way you can see your friends regularly when you come back."

"I'm going to give it at least a year, maybe two, here before I make any decisions. I've only been here three and a half months and I've been renovating for two of those months."

"That's true, but I detect some hostility in your voice about PEI. You know, I've been worried about you. I know you've been feeling depressed lately, and if you don't get out and make some friends you're just going to get more depressed."

There was that word again. Not once but twice. Mac was just starting to feel a little better until Dianna said the D-word. Fuck. Why did it upset him so much? Tell someone something long enough and they start to believe it, maybe? He was tempted to tell her he wasn't feeling depressed until she brought it up... tempted to say it in a terse tone. But then he realized, because he was feeling down, he was just hyper-sensitive to comments that described his mental health, even if they were... accurate?

"I'm not depressed. I just feel the isolation sometimes, I guess. I miss my friends too."

"I miss you too, honey. I think I know what you're going through. And don't take this the wrong way. I went through it. People don't understand unless they go through it. I'm just trying to help. If you put it in perspective, maybe you'll feel better."

Mac didn't think it would hurt. After all he had tried to think himself out of his funk earlier without much success. "Okay, what am I going through?"

"Culture shock."

"Culture shock? I'm still in Canada."

"It doesn't matter, Mac. I've been to PEI. The culture there is a *lot* different than Vancouver. There are four stages of culture shock. One, the honeymoon phase. You feel it when you first arrive. Everything's new and exciting. Life is a great adventure. Did you feel that?"

"Yes."

"Now the honeymoon's over, right?"

"I was just thinking that earlier today. What's stage two?"

"Hostility. Generally occurs a few months after you arrive. You start to realize the limitations of your new environment. You're far away from social venues, far away from your friends."

"What can I say? You nailed it."

"I'm not finished."

"Please, enlighten me."

"Don't be sarcastic."

"Okay."

"The symptoms of hostility are that you complain about a lot of things—you become highly critical of the locals. You might even say you hate the new environment, feel homesick and want to go home."

"Is there a light at the end of the tunnel?"

"I'm getting there. Stage three is humor. That's where you're starting to work through your negative feelings about the new culture. Maybe you've got new friends and you're coming to terms with the trade-offs of country living in PEI versus the big city of Vancouver."

"Maybe I'm stuck between hostility and humor. Sometimes I like the friendliness of Islanders."

"I don't think you believe that."

"You're probably right. Wasn't there a fourth stage?"

"The fourth and final stage is called home. That's where you accept your new home and you feel like you're there to stay."

"I'm not there yet."

"I know, and I'm worried about you."

"Don't Dianna."

"I can't help myself. You know how I am."

Mac knew. Dianna would give her last hundred dollars to a homeless person even if she didn't know where her next meal was coming from. But, as a highly successful sales representative for Bayer Pharmaceuticals, she didn't have that problem. She managed to juggle a successful ten-year marriage, three teenage kids, and a lucrative career with apparent ease, not to mention her many charitable undertakings.

"I'll be okay, I promise," Mac said.

"You'll call me if you need me, right?"

Mac doubted he would. "Of course."

"Just remember, you're going through the process of culture shock. If you know what's happening to you, sometimes it's easier to deal with."

"Thanks. I'm so grateful I have friends like you. I love you and miss you."

"I love you too. And I miss you. Have you made any plans for Christmas?"

"Nope."

"You can't just sit in your house alone on Christmas. You'll get really depressed."

Ugh... that word again, just when he was starting to feel better. "I'll think about it. I'll let you know."

"You better."

"Okay."

Mac explained a nasty storm was battering the property and he had to put away his plastic lawn furniture. He agreed to make plans for Christmas, promised to check in with her in a few days, and hung up.

A few minutes later, outside in whipping winds and blowing snow, collecting broken plastic chairs, he realized Dianna's explanation had cheered him a little and provided some perspective on what he was going through.

But it was the notion of Christmas without his parents and Ophelia that made his heart sink.

Chapter Three

December 13th—Friday the 13th—two days after the Ophelia disappointment in Montague, finishing up edits on the Voodoo witch website copy, Mac realized glumly that no, he didn't have any plans for Christmas.

He looked out into the blackness of the night. *No invites. No place to go.*

The blizzard had passed with only minor damage. Two plastic chairs and a table had been swooped into the trees by the wind and demolished. The storm had dumped twenty centimeters of snow, ripped down a few power poles and exploded a few electrical transformers on the Island. The result had been five hours without power, which meant no light, no internet, no water or heat. His only source of heat was an oil furnace, which required electricity to run. So he had gutted it out in bed in the wee hours of the morning, wrapped in thick blankets, until the power had been restored. A flickering candle had been his only source of heat, light and company.

By Thursday afternoon, crews had done an admirable job clearing roads. So, to try and stave off cabin fever and the dreaded D-word, Mac had ventured into Montague after sealing off some cracks in the basement sandstone foundation with some expanding spray foam insulation. He had driven by Petro Canada but, no, Ophelia's yellow Neon wasn't there. Whatever Ophelia's shifts were, Mac had yet to nail them down. So he had stopped off at the local Tim Horton's-slash-Wendy's, bought a large coffee, and sat by himself for an hour while locals came and went, some staring for a little longer than politeness allowed at the new kid on the block.

That made him feel more alone than ever, so he left, drove home, climbed into bed, and at 6:46 pm, fell into a deep sleep (one thing he did like about the country, most times he slept like a rock) waking at 6:30 this morning with the best intentions to stay happy today. He had cleaned the house, cooked a meal, read some excerpts from *Edgar Allan Poe's Complete Poetical Works,* shoveled a path to an outbuilding, affectionately named the man cave, and another to the barn where he parked the Dodge. Then, he had gotten to work on the edits for Maggie. But two hours later and making rather unsatisfactory progress, his mind drifted back to the dreaded Christmas. At one time in his life, it had been a joyous holiday, one that he looked forward to spending with his parents, Thomas and Margaret, who had lived in Calgary, Alberta.

That was before they died, December 13th, two years to the day. Mac glanced at the calendar and noticed the date for the first time. He frowned. No wonder the feeling of despair that had begun to envelop his mind, upon waking, was now descending like a black cloud. No wonder he hated Christmas. His parents, whom he had been very close to, had died in a car accident while driving to Vancouver to spend Christmas with him. A snowstorm had wreaked a path of devastation through Roger's Pass, while en route, and their mini-van careened off the road, flipped into the ditch, totaled the vehicle, and killed both of them on impact.

Mac still remembered the call from Constable Rod Billings like it was yesterday.

"Are you Mackenzie Adamson?"

He felt a rush of anxiety. "Yes."

"I'm sorry Mr. Adamson, I don't know any other way to tell you this. Your parents were killed in a single-vehicle accident at Roger's Pass early this morning."

"What? No, it can't be, no—"

"I'm very sorry. Do you have any other brothers or sisters?"

Fighting back tears, "Ah... no... no. I'm an only child."

"You might want to come and identify the bodies."

The rest of the conversation was vague. Between sobs, Mac told Constable Billings he would call him back later for the details.

He closed the Voodoo witch Word document and rubbed his temples, as if that might take away some of the pain. He didn't want to think about it right now, didn't want to relive all the grieving, for fear it would send him deeper into that helpless abyss of black depression. But the memory did answer some questions. Since his parents' death, every year in December he would feel their presence, grieve their loss, and wonder why he had changed his mind. Changed his mind about flying to Calgary for Christmas after Thomas had said it might be fun to escape the frigid cold and visit a more temperate climate like Vancouver over the holidays. Something sounded terribly wrong then, some sixth sense that Mac knew now he should have acted on. He should have just said no to his father's idea and booked a flight to Calgary. But his father, a retired oilfield mechanical engineer, had been rather insistent, telling Mac, "Your mother just loves the west coast, and she's getting awfully tired of minus forty. It would do her a world of good."

So Mac had agreed.

And now they were dead.

And sometimes the guilt was just too goddamned overwhelming. If he had just said no, they would be alive today. He knew now. He hated Christmas because he could no longer spend it with his parents. And all the Christmas trees, bells and whistles, rampant commercialism, jolly Santa Clauses, maniacal last-minute shoppers, joyful holiday music, snow and frigid temperatures did was remind him on some subtle but disturbing level of that terrible fact.

Everything was piling up and taking a toll on his mental health.

He was going through this struggle *alone* and *by himself*. There was no one around for miles. No friends here. What were his chances now of spending Christmas with Ophelia? Not good. Not good at all. But he felt he really needed some companionship for the holidays, otherwise the guilt, loneliness, isolation, that cursed D-word, might drive him right out of his mind.

Stark raving mad.

"Fuck Christmas."

He was answered by a scratching sound—something resembling nails on a chalkboard—behind him and inside the walls of his combination living-room, office and bedroom on the main floor of the old house.

Frightened, he spun around in his office chair and stared at the dark green wall.

Silence.

He stood up, put his ear to the wall, and listened.

Nothing.

Fuck it. It's your imagination. He left his office, wandered into the kitchen and made some coffee. While it perked, he went outside and stood on his back porch in the driving snow and wind and smoked. Sure, he liked cigarettes, but not enough to smoke them in his own house. He didn't like that stale and lingering smell. Besides, if he couldn't ultimately cut life on the "gentle" Island, how government tourism ads billed it, he could always list it for sale as a smoke-free house. In this day and age of political correctness, particularly in Canadian culture, smoking was almost as taboo as being addicted to heroin. Hell, heroin addicts probably got more sympathy and government hand-outs, methadone clinics for one, to help them kick the addiction.

After a few minutes, he returned to the kitchen and poured a cup of coffee.

Scratching, from inside the walls, almost like a ticking sound. *Ignore it. House is old. Has its creaks and groans.*

He fought an urge to run into the office from whence it came. Instead, he scooped up a half-teaspoon of sugar from the sugar bowl. He was about to drop it into his coffee when he stopped, staring wide-eyed at the spoon.

He gasped. There was a tiny mouse turd inside the spoon. He held it up to the light and examined it. Sure enough, mouse shit. Fuck. He threw the teaspoon of sugar and shit into the garbage can and checked the cupboards with a flashlight. No mouse shit. Then he carefully examined the kitchen counter, grimacing when he spotted two mouse turds. He lifted them carefully with some tissue paper (he had read Hantavirus, an airborne virus carried in mouse feces and urine, could be fatal) and dumped them into the garbage can.

The scraping sound resumed. *Click, click, ccccccccclick. Tick, tick, tick.*

He carried a kitchen chair and a flashlight up to the second floor and positioned it below the attic hatch. In preparation for winter, he had just had the attic insulation beefed up to R-50 with a blown-in fiberglass product. When the job was finished, he had asked one of the workers if he had seen any evidence of mice infestation.

"Definitely some holes up there, but they could be old. Have you heard anything in the walls?"

To which he'd answered in the negative. But that was before Old Man Winter had arrived. When the cold struck mice scrambled to get indoors and exterminator profits spiked accordingly. After removing the attic hatch, he shone the beam around. Sure enough, networks of tiny tunnels were visible in the two-foot high white insulation fibers. *Fuck, they're in the walls. How are they getting into the kitchen?*

******

Two hours later, Mac was still not completely satisfied with his efforts. He knew the mice must have come in through the crawl-space basement, accessible only from an outside door. But, with over two feet of snow outside and a nasty storm, it would have to do for now. He had sealed off two cold air vents with duct-taped screens, cut a square piece of plywood and screwed it to a chimney flue opening in the dining room wall, and set three mousetraps with peanut butter in the kitchen along the baseboards, where he knew the critters traveled. He had read mice can get into a crack a quarter-inch high and less than an inch wide. Prior to the duct-taping and aluminum screen patch job, the air vents in the floor had openings at least that big. When the weather improved, he would have to make a concerted effort to seal off the house, double-check the insulation job he had done in the basement foundation cracks, and plant plenty of poison bait stations in the kitchen, attic and basement. If that didn't work, he would call in the exterminators and declare all-out war on the little bastards.

To drown out the creepy sound of the vermin crawling inside his bedroom walls, Mac had turned on the radio and sat listening to weather reports. Thankfully, his power hadn't gone out. Yet. He still had heat, internet, and of course the trusty cell phone, which fortunately didn't depend on hard-wired connections.

He listened to a weather report on CBC radio: "Parts of a winter storm hitting the Maritimes have turned to rain, creating black ice on the roads and sparking police requests for motorists to stay home..."

Surfing the internet, he came across a warning issued by the government of Canada, specific to King's Country, where he lived: *This is a warning that dangerous winter weather conditions are affecting Prince Edward Island. Monitor weather conditions and listen for updated statements. An intensifying low pressure system will pass over Nova Scotia later this evening to lie over Newfoundland Monday morning. This system is expected to bring heavy snow and strong easterly winds. Total snowfall amounts of 25 to 35 centimeters are expected across the province, accompanied by strong easterly winds of up to 80 km/h, giving reduced visibilities due to blowing snow. Higher than normal water levels and rough pounding surf can be expected this evening at high tide. Those planning travel or other weather-sensitive activities are advised to monitor future forecasts and warnings.*

Even if he did have friends on the Island, Mac couldn't go anywhere in this weather. And he didn't fancy talking on the phone to any of his Vancouver friends, remembering Eric Clapton's lyrics: *Nobody loves you when you're down and out.*

So he switched off his two laptops, turned off the radio, and went to bed. It was a long time before he fell asleep. His thoughts drifted to the mice. He could hear them inside the walls scurrying up and down, making an annoying scraping, clicking and ticking sound. His mind floated to the isolation and his ill-fated attempts at making friends and dating Ophelia. The black cloud came floating in. Outside, the wind howled, lashing snow against the house, causing it to creak and groan.

The mice continued their infernal clicking.

Finally, he became dozy. He felt something crawling across his head. He leaped out of bed and switched the bedside lamp on frantically, almost knocking it over. He searched around. After a panicked moment, dry-mouthed, heart thumping in chest, he realized it was a blanket fold that had fallen on his ear.

CLACK!

The sound from the kitchen startled him. He went in with a flashlight. A mousetrap had slammed shut on a mouse's neck. Its black eyes bulged from the sockets and a small drool of blood dribbled from its mouth. It wriggled for a few seconds then fell still.

"Gotcha you little fuck."

Grabbing a coat and gloves, Mac took the mousetrap outside, deposited the mouse into a driveway ditch and returned to bed. He didn't bother reloading the trap. There were two more ready to kill anyway.

As he lay in bed, he thought of how he could turn his funk around, before it got so strong as to prevent him from working, socializing, hell, functioning at all. Then it came to him. Or rather, she came to him. Three weeks prior to leaving Vancouver, he had met realtor Carla Pedersen at a coffee shop. The conversation they had struck up resulted in a dinner-date.

Carla was a forty-something slim blonde with striking blue eyes. Over dinner, she explained to Mac that her last common-law husband, who had lived with her in her house for six years, had developed three addictions, during their last two years together; boozing, internet porn-surfing and gambling. Bill Roddenberry had convinced Carla that he could use her savings, $200,000, and the equity in her home, $250,000, and make a mountain of money with it. Carla had agreed. Needless to say he had lost all the money and Carla. She had kicked him out of her house and went through a nasty court battle just to keep it. Motivated by this disaster, she had vowed to work like a dog, become mortgage-free and accumulate another $200,000 savings in five years. The result, using her words, was, "I don't go out, I haven't dated in two years, I work all the time and my colleagues tell me to get a life."

"It's an admirable goal," Mac had said. "But are you happy?"

He thought he saw a shadow pass over her blue eyes before her expression brightened. "I'm working hard now to be happy tomorrow."

"But tomorrow might never come."

She sighed. "Maybe you're right."

After dinner, there was an awkward moment in the parking lot outside the restaurant, as if neither of them quite wanted to go their separate ways but also didn't want to admit it.

Finally, they decided to go to Carla's for one glass of wine.

"But you can't sleep over."

One glass of wine led to two, then three, then four. They sat on lawn chairs in Carla's back deck, facing a pastoral field, watching the sunset and enjoying the warm summer breeze. The conversation was easy, relaxed and funny. Finally, Mac felt sure he was overstaying his welcome and announced he was leaving. It was ten-thirty and they both had to work the next day. He moved in for a quick hug, a short peck on the cheek. It turned into a long, passionate embrace and a one-minute necking session.

"I better go," Mac said finally. Otherwise I *will* sleep over."

The next day they exchanged many text messages. It's just what people do now. They don't talk. They text. The day after that, the texting bordered on sexting. And on the third day, Mac had called Carla and asked her out on another date, inviting her to his downtown condo for "nothing fancy, just pizza and home-made wine."

She had agreed, even bringing pizza. After eating, they retreated to the enclosed balcony, watching the twinkling city lights below, drinking wine, smoking and chatting. Then things turned more intimate. Mac leaned in for a kiss and the next thing he knew Carla was sitting on his lap. They necked and their hands roamed teasingly. That's when Mac realized it wasn't right. He probably could have gone all the way, but he had more respect for her than that. He was leaving and she knew it.

On the first date she had even said off-handedly, "I'm not moving to PEI with you, you know."

Mac didn't know what to make of the comment so he just let it go. He didn't want a long-distance relationship and he knew, neither did Carla.

He stopped. "I don't think this is right, Carla. I have more respect for you."

She nodded. "I don't want to get hurt anymore. And you're leaving. What are you doing with me anyway?"

"I don't know. I like you."

"I like you too. I'll miss you."

"I just thought if I like someone, shouldn't I try and see them, without automatically dismissing the thought just because I'm leaving? I don't know, Carla. What can I say? I like you so I wanted to see you, maybe wanted to see where it would go."

"Where can it go? I'm not moving to PEI and you probably won't be coming back here."

Mac wasn't about to change his plans. Not after two years in the making. "I guess you're right. I don't know what I was thinking."

Carla removed herself from his lap and they continued talking about relationships. Mac told her his accomplishments in editing just didn't mean anything anymore; they felt empty if he didn't have someone to share them with. "I want someone to celebrate my accomplishments with me as a part of theirs. Things I couldn't do without their support."

Carla admitted that her financial goals, at the expense of her personal life and happiness, seemed so shallow and empty at times. She confessed to suffering from terrible anxiety occasionally and even took prescription sleeping pills and Ativan.

Mac had admitted to being a part-time insomniac but said he rarely suffered from severe anxiety or depression.

As if she could foresee the future, she pulled out a pill bottle of Ativan and rolled five of them onto the coffee table. "Here. You can have them. You take one of these little pills and all your problems seem unimportant."

Not wanting to seem rude, Mac accepted the pills, thinking he would flush them down the toilet as soon as Carla left.

They talked about the possibility of Carla visiting him in PEI and about taking a tropical holiday together to get a reprieve from the cold Canadian winters.

"Keep in touch," she said. "E-mail some before and after pictures of the home renovations and let's see what the future brings."

That was the last time he saw her.

On August 15th, a day after arriving on the Island, he was feeling out of sorts about the entire move and called Carla.

"Don't worry, it's natural— after such a big move—to feel lonely and homesick," she said. "We'll talk soon."

Something in her tone said they wouldn't. And they hadn't. It was now over three months since he had any contact with Carla. But he still thought about her about twice a week and often wondered if he should call her.

But he threw himself into home renovations and forgot about her. The summer weather was beautiful, the ocean was inspirational, and the animals were amazing. *The honeymoon's over.* After two months of renovating, he thought about her again. But he chickened out on the call, instead sending her an e-mail and five pictures of the property. The e-mail was friendly, updating her on his progress and the idiosyncrasies of Island culture. He had ended it with: *I hope to talk to you real soon and catch up. Have an awesome day.*

A day went by and no response to the e-mail. A week went by. Nothing. Now it had been three months and he hadn't heard anything from Carla. *That's just the fucking problem with e-mail.* He snarled. You don't know if it ended up in a spam folder, or maybe she got pissed off because she thought she deserved at least a phone call. Maybe she's got another boyfriend. Maybe she received it and misunderstood its meaning. Maybe she found something derogatory in what Mac thought was a perfectly polite, even carefully-worded greeting. Oh let's face it, there were many possibilities.

Thinking about Carla had made Mac more awake than ever. He was tossing and turning now. Because, regardless of the possibilities, there was only one way to see it. Another rejection. First that landscaping loser. Then that Texas flake. Then the dance hall freak. And now Carla.

Three strikes yer out... four strikes yer fucked. Yer fucked now.

He remembered the Ativan, which he hadn't disposed of after all but saved for a rainy day, or in this case a fucking snowstorm. No time like the present. He went into the bathroom, found the pill bottle in the medicine cabinet, swallowed a little white pill with a mouthful of water and returned to his office. He fired up a laptop and googled it, just so he knew what he was taking, realizing the irony of the situation; mice in the attic, and he, a laboratory mouse in his own mental experiment. He sighed. Next it would be bats in the belfry if he wasn't careful.

Wikipedia described the drug as a "high-potency, intermediate duration drug used for the short-term treatment of anxiety, insomnia, acute seizures... and sedation of hospitalized patients, as well as sedation of aggressive patients...It is also the most common benzodiazepine used to decrease the likelihood of agitation and seizures in patients who have overdosed on stimulant drugs."

Another website, DRUGS.COM warned, "Ativan may be habit-forming and should be used only by the person it was prescribed for. Ativan should never be shared with another person, especially someone who has a history of drug abuse or addiction. Keep the medication in a secure place where others cannot get to it."

Even before finishing the brief research, Mac felt the drug's effects. The black cloud was there alright, but it was weakening, turning light gray. He turned off the computer and returned to bed.

The scratching of the mice started. But it didn't seem as bad.

"Don't worry you motherfuckers, tomorrow's all-out war."

He closed his eyes and began to feel the sedative effects whilst trying not to think of anything at all. Twenty minutes later the black cloud turned white. But his eyelids were getting heavy and the blackness of sleep was creeping into his subconscious.

He drifted off and dreamed.

The surroundings were blurry, indiscernible, somewhere on the periphery. He entered a classroom to listen to a lecture on a subject he knew not. The teacher started and finished the lecture and Mac didn't understand a single word she said. Or, he didn't want to know. He was high up in the back row. And as the instructor talked, he noticed Carla sitting in the front row taking copious notes. Then he realized. It was a real estate seminar. She was a realtor. That's why she was there.

But what was he doing there?

She acknowledged him with a perfunctory wave and returned her attention to the lecture.

All the agonizing thoughts about rejection surfaced while he wriggled and squirmed uncomfortably, knowing, but not knowing why he couldn't leave until it was over.

It ended.

On the way out, he passed Carla, standing by the door. He said a quick hello, feeling a blush spread across his cheeks. *How do I handle this? What if she blows me off?* Men and rejection. Not a good combination.

He stopped and turned around. Other people were filing out and talking. Carla looked at him.

Mac felt the blush grow hotter on his cheeks. "It's been so long. How are you?"

She curled a finger.

He approached her.

"I've been struggling, Mac. My life is empty, without meaning. What about you?"

He nodded. "The same."

He put his hands in his pockets and his head down.

"Do you still like me?" she asked.

He raised his head, made slight eye contact and glanced to the floor again.

"Yes."

"I like you too."

He raised his head slowly, locking eyes with Carla. "Do you? I didn't think so. I didn't hear back."

"Forget the past," she said, a slow and confident smile forming. "We need to be together. You need to be with me. I need to be with you. Do you feel that way?"

"Yes."

He moved closer, arms outstretched, closing his eyes as he prepared for the hug, the accompanying passionate kiss. Happily ever after. But he hugged and kissed thin air, his eyes popped open and he bolted up in bed, drenched in sweat. His heart was beating normally, but he was cold. Soaking wet and shivering. Even the sheets were wet. He got up and relieved himself, changed clothes, changed sheets, and returned to bed, where he tossed and turned for a long time before falling asleep. When he finally did drift off, he dreamed of a million mice crawling out of a million holes in the walls, nibbling on his ears, nose, eyes and entire body. He writhed, screamed in terror and woke up. His heart was pounding in his chest. He was scared. But at least he wasn't drenched in his own sweat. So he lay awake for a long time listening to the mice make steady progress up and down the inside of the wall—the inside of his head—before finally falling into a deep and dreamless sleep.

Chapter Four

Waking that Saturday morning, December 14^{th,} Mac remembered the Carla dream as if it were real. He knew exactly what he had to do. He had to call Carla. What was he thinking with Ophelia anyway? Sure he wanted a local woman, not a long-distance relationship, but Ophelia was at least half his age. Not to mention the fucking gas station, a next to impossible venue to ever make contact. And he didn't even know her. At least Carla was his age and he knew her. He felt like there was a connection, despite the distance factor.

He relieved himself and went outside to smoke. The sun was shining. It was chilly but calm and windless. The storm had dumped at least a foot of snow. He heard a squawk and looked at his apple tree. Two partridges, perched on branches, were eating tree buds. A bald eagle soared overhead. He lit a cigarette. *I should be able to drive the Dodge through the snow without a snowplow*. He returned inside the house and went into the kitchen, with the intention of calling Carla later.

He examined the two traps closely. Both were missing the peanut butter bait but had not sprung.

"Fucking bastards...I'll get you today."

He checked the kitchen counter. Two more mouse droppings. He carefully removed them, cleaned the counter with disinfectant, and prepared coffee. After his second cup, he returned to his computer. He would work on the Voodoo witch edits for a couple of hours then head into Montague to buy some ammunition for the devolving mouse war.

Opening up the document, his mind drifted. He realized the black cloud had not come. Despite the mouse nightmare, which he also remembered vividly, he had slept rather well. For a change, he felt rather refreshed and alive. He just hoped the black cloud wouldn't visit later in the day. Last night, he had counted the Ativan, just in case. Four pills remaining. He didn't want to become dependent on them, just use one or two to help him get over the hump. Then his biological preservation systems would kick in and take him the rest of the way home. That was the hope.

He minimized the website document and checked his e-mail. He stopped at a message from Maggie, the Voodoo witch. The heading—URGENT—had caught his eye:

Dear Mac, Thanks so much for editing my website copy. I know you'll do a great job. I appreciate the discount. I had a vision of you last night. I know you're lonely and looking for a woman. I can cast a spell on you from Skype to help you get the woman of your dreams. And it's free, as I promised. Don't tell me, I already know. It's Ophelia. Please Skype me as soon as possible. Your happy future depends on it. Your Voodoo witch in the Caribbean, Maggie.

Mac puzzled over the e-mail. He had told Maggie during the initial consultation he was single, but nothing else. How did she know he was lonely? How did she know about Ophelia? Vision? What vision? One part of him wanted to put the theory to the test. Although he'd always been curious about mediums, clairvoyants, psychics, witches, whatever your want to call them, he didn't know how much stock to put into their practices. On the one hand, he wasn't eager to dismiss them; on the other, he wasn't eager to embrace them. Ambivalent maybe.

Put it to the test. What can it hurt? But another part of him, the part that had a healthy respect for the unknown, the part that maybe even had a healthy fear of the unknown, cautioned him to stay away. And now that he had dreamt about Carla last night, he wasn't even sure of his feelings about Ophelia anymore.

He typed a quick e-mail to Maggie, telling her he was going into town to run some errands. He promised to think about her offer and discuss it in a few hours. There were a few points of clarification he needed on her website anyway, points that would be cleared up much quicker through a conversation versus e-mail. Sometimes, in e-mail, shit just gets lost in translation, particularly when you're dealing with someone whose native tongue is Spanish and not English. Never mind that, it happens often enough with native English speakers too. Electronic communication and social media equals the death of conversation. A phone call was the way to go.

He spent a few hours editing Maggie's copy and scribbling notes. May as well make the most efficient use of the call. He wrote a list of supplies he needed in Montague and was about to leave the house. Suddenly, he stopped in his tracks and turned back. Carla. Time to call Carla. A call would tell him if his dream was real—a premonition dream. Then, if he did take Maggie up on her offer, maybe he could use the spell to acquire Carla instead.

Surely she wouldn't reject him. Not another one. Please not another one. Dialing her number, he felt the butterflies tickling his stomach. Some crawled along his spine and his flesh broke out in goose bumps. He really was nervous.

She said hello on the first ring.

"Carla, it's Mac."

"Well, hello there stranger, how are you?"

Mac sighed. He could tell from her tone she still liked him. There was still a mutual attraction.

They got through the preliminary small talk.

Mac said, "I sent you an e-mail a while back with some photos of the acreage. Did you get it?"

"I did. And I'm sorry I didn't respond. You know I had all the best intentions, even started crafting a well-worded response. Then it ended up in my drafts and I guess I forgot about it."

Mac sighed. *No rejection this time. No strike-out yet. Batter's on the plate, 'bout to hit a home run, Clyde.*

"It's okay, Carla. I figured something like that happened, but I have to admit, I started to wonder. I thought maybe you were pissed off because I e-mailed instead of calling. You know when you don't hear from someone your mind starts to spin out all kinds of scenarios."

"It was nothing like that. I'm glad to hear from you."

Carla told Mac about the active real estate market and how she was busy closing multiple deals. Mac filled her in on PEI life, renovations, his lack of a social life, the isolation, how he found country living on the other hand very peaceful and inspirational, how he was doing well with his editing and SEO writing business, reading lots of books and even spending a little time doing some creative writing. Then he asked her if she had any plans for Christmas.

"I hate Christmas. I'm spending it with my two sisters, their husbands, five kids, and my mother and father. I wish it would just pass by so I can get back to work."

"Yeah, but Carla, those are people you love. That's not so bad."

"It *is* bad. I go there and they're all happy and shit and then I compare them to my life and realize how empty it is. Christmas can be very tough for single people you know."

Mac remembered his dead parents and swallowed a lump of sorrow. "You don't have to convince me. I'm not a fan of Christmas. You don't have a boyfriend to invite along?"

"No, I had one, after you left. We dated for a few months. He dumped me. Guess I'm not very good at relationships."

That would explain the lack of response on the e-mail. Maybe she was heartsick. "I'm sorry to hear that Carla. That must be hard. I wouldn't dump you."

"But you live on the east coast and I live on the west coast."

"I know."

"And thanks. It was hard, but I'm getting over it. At least it wasn't three years."

Enough with the questions already, she's probably still grieving over the split. "Are you happy, in general, in Vancouver?" *She just got dumped you fucking bonehead.*

"I'm lonely just like you. Sometimes work fills in the void and sometimes it doesn't. And when it doesn't, I can't sleep and get anxious."

Mac remembered the Ativan. "I'm sorry to hear it. You know I'm a part-time insomniac. When I first arrived here, I had a hard time sleeping. Maybe two months it lasted. Now finally I think I've adjusted to the house." Mac thought about the mice nibbling on him and shuddered. "Because most times I sleep like a rock here."

"That's good. What're you doing for Christmas anyway?"

"No plans."

"Do you think you'll last there?"

"I don't know. But I'm not going to make any rash decisions until I've been here for at least a year, maybe two."

"That's a good idea. Maybe when you settle in you'll like it."

"I love it in the summer, but I'm not a fan of winter. You know, when I first arrived, I thought I could gut out a winter here, depend on my resolves. But I forgot about my need for human companionship."

"I've done that before. I'm doing it now. I'm all about work and sometimes my life feels so lonely and empty."

"For me, sometimes it feels as if the idyllic-country-life dream is turning into a nightmare."

"But it's beautiful there. I saw the pictures. Your beachfront. The forest. All the animals."

The conversation made itself for a while and then gaps started to form. Carla probably had work to do. He better not keep her. Just as he was about to offer her an out, something like "I better not keep you, I'm sure you've got plenty of work to do," he suddenly had an urge to tell her about the dream. Never mind *the* dream; come to think of it, it was the third time he had dreamt about Carla. "You know I dreamt of you last night?"

"You dreamt of me?"

"Yeah."

"Maybe I shouldn't ask what it was about. Maybe I don't want to know."

"It wasn't sexual, Carla."

"Was it a nightmare?"

"No. Do you want to know what it was about?"

Silence.

"Come on, Carla, I know your women's curiosity is getting the better of you. Even if it was sexual, you'd probably want to hear all about it."

Mac thought the conversation had become remarkably candid, remarkably fast.

She laughed.

"Maybe if it was sexual I *would* want you to tell me. Or write it out. You're a creative type."

"If I wrote it, I think you'd like it."

"Maybe I would. Maybe I'd want you to write it and read it to me. Maybe I'd like it even better then."

"I'd do a good job. I didn't coin it but writing is refined thinking. I'd have a lot more time to pick the right words to describe the action. You know, tantalizing stuff."

"Just tell me already."

Mac explained the details, saying the dream had left him feeling happy that she still wanted to connect with him, still smiled at him. He also said he'd had at least three similar dreams, omitting that one of them had indeed been rather sexual. "When I woke up I also knew that I just had to call you."

"I like you, Mac. You're a great guy and easy to talk to."

"Thanks. I like you too."

Carla promised to be more forthcoming with her e-mail responses. They even revisited the notion of taking a tropical vacation together sometime in the near future.

"I would wish you a Merry Christmas but I know how you feel about the holidays," Mac said. "So how's enjoy the holiday season?"

"That'll do. And same to you."

"You know how I tell my good friends Merry Christmas, the ones who get my twisted sense of humor and know I'm not a fan of the holiday?"

"How?"

"Merry fucking Xmas."

"You can tell it to me like that."

"Merry fucking Xmas, Carla."

"Merry fucking Xmas to you."

"Thank you. Sometimes I e-mail greeting cards to my close friends. I put some bullshit about how I wish them everlasting peace, joy and a glee-filled holiday. You know, all the best to you and yours on this very special occasion, blah, blah, blah... some sentimental shit. Then they scroll down to a picture of me flipping the double-bird. Sometimes even a blurb at the bottom of the photo... Fuck Christmas and fuck you... something like that. Or merry fucking Xmas and fuck you in the New Year."

"A man after my own heart."

"You can't be serious?"

******

Fifteen minutes later, driving along well-ploughed roads (the trusty Dodge had been successful after all in making tracks out of Mac's snow-covered driveway without the aid of a snowplow), Mac felt almost giddy with excitement. He hadn't felt like this in a long time. But as he turned onto Main Street Montague, a few minutes later, having rehashed and analyzed the important snippets of the conversation—*she still likes me*—his happiness turned to confusion.

All those thoughts he had about Ophelia came flooding back. He had gone so far as to envision a perfect white-picket-fence life with her. The images swirled in his mind; kissing her, laughing with her, cuddling up with her on the couch on a cold winter's night and watching a movie. Making love with her.

He suddenly realized with a growing certainty and unease he was going to accept Maggie's offer.

The question was who would be the beneficiary of the magic love spell?

Chapter Five

Seeing Ophelia again, Mac hoped for some magic intervention. He hadn't done that well on his own. He had run his errands in Montague, purchased two large boxes of mouse poison, two sticky traps, two cans of spray foam for basement cracks, a jar of peanut butter for the more conventional traps, and filled up with gas. Ophelia wasn't at the gas station. But when he stopped at the local Subway, he saw her sitting by the window with a female friend, chatting and eating lunch.

She even turned her head and smiled at him. Mac smiled back.

Nervously standing in line, he rehearsed a possible dialogue. If only he could work up the courage to approach her table and even say hello. I could sure use some help here. Some magic. *Let's see, she's sitting with a friend. That makes it difficult right there. Okay, here goes. Go over, at least say hello, comment on the storm, all the snow; that another storm is on its way tonight. Once the small talk stops, hand her your business card, say, "I'm new to the Island. It would be great to get together with you for a coffee or something, sometime." How are you going to do that when her friend is right there, staring at you, making you uncomfortable? Just do it, like Nike says. Do you want to be taking another Ativan tonight? Do it. What can I get you?*

"What can I get you?"

Mac blinked, realizing the question wasn't in his head. The female sandwich-maker had spoken. He looked at her blankly for a moment, glancing behind and seeing a mildly annoyed beefy man waiting impatiently for him to order. How long had he been standing there daydreaming? He didn't know. He ordered quickly and took his sandwich, the woman giving him one of those *Are you okay?* looks as he walked away with his cold-cut combo toasted submarine sandwich on Italian bread.

There were three empty tables along the window in the corner where Ophelia sat. A few others were occupied by customers. Mac walked down the aisle toward her. He paused beside her and glanced at her. "How are you?"

A few heads turned.

She looked at him and smiled. "Oh, hi. I'm good."

Mac returned the smile. That was that. He chickened out, walked past her and sat by the window a few tables down and ate his sub.

In a public restaurant with other customers and her friend around it just wasn't an easy proposition. But, somehow, he didn't feel deflated and depressed, like after the last encounter with Ophelia. The conversation with Carla had lifted his spirits somewhat and Maggie's offer still churned around in his head.

Ophelia and her friend finished their meals and left, without acknowledging that Mac even existed, not as if they should.

Mac wasn't dismayed. *Magic will do it. Magic will give me the edge I need.*

******

A few hours later, after driving home through a storm, Mac was surfing the internet.

Since Maggie practiced Haitian Voodoo, the dominant religion of Haiti, Mac focused his efforts there. Thinking

Voodoo was nothing more than rank superstition, he was surprised to learn Voodoo was taken very seriously by many intelligent and learned followers. Haitian Voodoo, practiced for centuries as a religion, was brought to the Caribbean by Africans, during the slave trade. After years of suppression, Voodoo was recognized as a religion in the 1990s and has grown to about sixty million followers today. There is only one God, Bondye, the Supreme Being, similar to the God of Christianity and other western religions. Voodoo worship often involves animal sacrifice, incantations, dance and communication with and possession by spirits, or Loa.

Loa, who interact with the people of the Earth, are the spirits of family members and the major forces of the universe. They represent good and evil, health and reproduction, and all aspects of daily life. During religious ceremonies, Loa mount or possess people, causing good and bad things to happen to them. The notion of free will is foreign to the believer. Whatever happens to an individual, it is the Loa who have caused it.

Becoming absorbed in his research, Mac surfed on. He learned Voodoo is divided into two types, Rada and Petro. Rada, accounting for 95 per cent of Haitian Voodoo, is practiced for healing, pacifying the spirits, the initiation of new priests or priestesses, interpreting dreams, casting protective spells and creating potions for purposes primarily concerned with good. The Rada Loa are peaceful and happy while the Petro represent the evil five per cent. Dangerous things happen in Petro black magic Voodoo, including death spells, zombification and wild sexual orgies.

Mac found a lot of conflicting information: one African witch doctor on You Tube claimed that Voodoo does not do evil things; it heals the community's sick, brings peace, happiness and general well-being to its followers. The witch doctor went on to say that some children are born with spiritual powers. Those children, in some cases feared by elders, must not be insulted or beaten by parents. If the parents follow the rules (he never specified exactly what the rules were) raising the children, all will be well. If they don't, the mother or father will die.

Another Voodoo magic website claimed its potent spells have the ability to heal but also end lives, warning potential customers that only the most serious cases will be considered and its spells are not for playful experimentation. A list of spells included stopping your partner from cheating, finding the love of your life, and even placing a curse on an enemy.

Reading, Mac noticed a sudden chill in the room, stood up, and checked the thermostat. It read twenty degrees Celsius, just like it should. His feet were suddenly cold. Prickly spears poked his back. He put on a pair of thick wool socks, went to the back porch, opened the door, went outside and lit a smoke. It was bitterly cold with three-foot snow drifts already starting to accumulate around the outbuildings. A crow landed on an apple tree next to the property, its eyes glittering red from the porch light, seemingly oblivious to the weather. It eyeballed him, cawed angrily, and flew away.

Mac returned to the computer and continued to surf. Although he didn't want to acknowledge it, he realized the black cloud of depression was being replaced by something much worse— raw fear.

He found another blog post by a witch doctor, instructing readers how to kill someone by casting an evil "black magic" spell. Gather one of their possessions. Find a moonlit place and make a magic circle of protection. Make a flammable doll of the victim. Light a candle or two. Draw a satanic symbol (baphamet) in the circle, place the doll in it and invoke Abaddon the destroyer, whilst directing all your rage and hatred against your enemy. Plunge needles into the doll—abdomen, head and heart, slit the doll from head to groin with a knife and set it on fire. Bye, bye enemy.

When you're finished, "Go have a beer. After all, you deserve it. You just set in motion the demise of your most hated enemy. While the curse might not take effect right away, the seed you have placed will take root and grow. And you'll probably feel much better after casting the spell."

Mac closed the website and shuddered. He was suddenly cold again. The thermostat still read twenty.

Morbid curiosity pushed him on. He discovered other stories about Voodoo misuse:

A woman in the United States hired a Voodoo priest to perform a good-luck ritual. They lit candles. He had sex with her. During the distraction, the candles sparked a fire, killing one resident and injuring eleven in an apartment building.

Performing a Haitian Voodoo ritual, a mother and grandmother set a six-year-old girl on fire, causing second and third-degree burns to twenty-five per cent of her body.

Accused of spreading a cholera outbreak that killed at least 2,500 in Haiti, angry mobs stoned and hacked to death with machetes 45 Voodoo priests or houngans.

A New York man bludgeoned his mother-in-law to death with a steel pipe, claiming "she was trying to hex me" with Voodoo dust.

But one story, perhaps the most macabre, caused another cold draft in the office. He was sure he even saw a note pinned to a bulletin board flutter from it.

In 2011, a boat, packed with 400 people departed Libya bound for the Italian island of Lampedusa. Seas grew stormy. Several Nigerian women allegedly began an eerie Voodoo-style dance, chanting to the spirits to calm the stormy waters threatening to capsize the boat. Apparently, as a sacrifice to the devil, twelve illegal immigrants were thrown overboard, at least one beaten badly prior to meeting a watery grave.

Mac's heart began to beat faster. His mouth went dry. He took a few deep breaths, closed the windows, turned off the computer, went outside to the back porch, lit another cigarette, and paced nervously. The blizzard was unleashing its fury. Over two feet of snow had fallen. It was just before six at night, but the sky was a starless, moonless, dark gray haze.

Oblivious to the storm, a crow flew out of nowhere, circled Mac's head, cawed angrily and disappeared. It flew so close he could feel the rush of air from the fluttering wings. Startled, Mac jumped back, slipping on the frosty surface and almost falling into a snow drift.

He crushed his cigarette out. He gripped the screen door handle with both hands and pulled on it, as the wind threatened to bash and unhinge it. He finally got it open, closed it, and shut himself inside.

The short exposure to the blizzard had left him cold and the minimal internet research had left him even colder—with terror.

He didn't call Maggie that evening. Instead he went to bed early, without taking the Ativan as he had intended. He listened to the hissing wind battering the house and the tick, tick, tick of the mice making steady progress inside the walls. But earlier, he had put six poison bait stations in the attic, another six in the basement, and two in the kitchen. He hoped the mice were feeding on the poison and going to their deaths. But the incessant scraping was irritating and sleep did not come easily. And when it did it was a thin, restless sleep. But in the wee hours of the morning, sleep took hold and dragged him down to a deep level of REM, where he dreamed.

He was in an Indian village somewhere. Drums beat while natives chanted and danced around a small fire. A dark-skinned spear-toting man led the group. His face and body was smeared with splashes of orange, yellow, red, white and black. The drums stopped suddenly. Narrowing his blood-red eyes to slits, the man raised the spear and turned to Mac.

The blood-red eyes of the congregants followed the priest's gaze. He opened his mouth, uttered a guttural shriek and pounded his chest, looking into the full moon and the black starlit sky. He stopped, his scrutiny returning to Mac.

"It's a sad day for our village," he said, his biceps swelling as he wept black tears. "You must die."

"You must die," the villagers chanted in unison, their voices rising to a crescendo.

Fear penetrated Mac's heart like a black spear.

With his heart pounding and beads of sweat springing up on his forehead, he leaped to his feet. "No, it's not supposed to be like this."

The drums started beating.

The chant—"You must die!"—continued.

Mac turned to run, immediately thinking he would be frozen to the spot. But, no, his legs carried him off into the jungle. *Twang!* A spear struck a palm tree, narrowly missing him. Chased by chanting native Indians, he ran into the jungle, found a path, and continued running. Running, running, running.

A short time later, he stopped, panting for breath, and listened. The sound of footfalls, swishing of branches, chanting, grew louder. They were nearing—coming to get him, coming to kill him.

And the fear was almost paralyzing.

He turned to run, but stopped. The jungle had suddenly grown around him. The trail had disappeared and he was surrounded by dense foliage.

The footfalls neared.

His heart raced. *Thump-thump-thump-thump-thump thump thump.*

Then he saw it, at least a hundred black spears, dimly lit by the moon, approaching, coming to stab him again and again.

A black ball of terror rising in his chest, he cried out. "NO, NO, SOMEONE HELP ME!"

A voice called out, as if God had answered his call. "In here, quick."

He looked. A hand reached out from the dense foliage, its owner lost in the blackness. The voice. He knew that voice. It was an effort to speak. The fear. The dry mouth. "Maggie?"

"It's me. Take my hand."

He grabbed the hand. It was warm to the touch. And, as the spears approached, he noticed some tiny droplets of dark red blood on the helping hand. Then he floated above the jungle, up and away, melding, becoming one with the darkness. The fear faded, slowly replaced by an uneasy black calm.

The woman behind the hand was shrouded in blackness. But he knew it was Maggie. And he knew he was safe. Because what she said reassured him.

"I'm here to save you. Fear not."

Chapter Six

Put aside the fear, Mac told himself. Fear not.

"Is this going to hurt?" he asked the microphone inside his laptop computer.

"No," Maggie said. "It won't a hurt a bit. It's going to help you a lot."

Just over a week had passed since the storm of Saturday, December 14th. Now, Sunday afternoon, December 22nd—three days before Christmas—Mac had finally acquiesced to the free spell. Maybe it was the nightmare—"*I'm here to save you. Fear not*"—that had convinced him. Maybe it was the loneliness and depression that had started to creep back in after he had finished with Maggie's website copy, been paid in full, and had told her respectfully, "Thanks for the offer, but I think I'll pass all the same."

He had used up the Ativan and wasn't getting a lot of relief from the demons of depression.

Maybe it was the lack of female companionship. So close to Christmas, and Mac still had not managed to land a date with Ophelia. Carla had just left to Mexico for a two-week all-inclusive vacation. Mac had sat on the fence too long and she had departed.

Maybe it was the relentless storms battering the Island. Mac glanced out his window as snow fell down. Fifteen centimeters on the way, with fifty kilometer winds. And the snow was supposed to turn into freezing pellets by the evening, making the entire Island one giant skating rink.

Or maybe it was because Maggie had been so persistent, calling three times in the last week, asking if he had changed his mind. Mac didn't know anymore. And he didn't care. He was at the point where he would do almost anything for a companion.

But he was still a little suspicious.

"This isn't black magic?" he asked the computer nervously.

Maggie had her video-camera turned off. Her website only contained an animated caricature of a young, black-haired gypsy woman, a colorful bandanna wrapped around her head. Mac had no idea what she looked like, and she had made it clear, she did not wish to reveal her identity. Yet. Returning the favor, Mac had his video-camera turned off. Two could play at that game.

"No," she said. "It's white magic. Should we begin?"

Since Carla's departure, Mac had chosen Ophelia for the love spell. Carla was in Mexico anyway and Maggie's vision involved Ophelia. She was the chosen one. Why fight fate?

"You sure we can do this over Skype?" Mac said.

"Oh yes. Magic transcends boundaries."

He sighed deeply. A decision had been made that would change the course of his destiny forever. His office door creaked open. He jerked his head, stood up, and closed it. Goose bumps appeared on his arms. He sat down, shuddering.

"Are you okay?" Maggie asked.

"Let's get this over with."

"Okay, I'm turning the video on."

A fiery orange image illuminated for a second and then blackness enveloped the screen. A candle-lit red inverted pentagram swung into view.

"Keep your eyes on it," Maggie said. "Blank your mind and watch it."

The pentagram swayed back and forth. A soundtrack, barely audible at first, but growing louder, played. It was eerily similar to Alfred Hitchcock's movie *Psycho*. Mac shivered and returned his attention to the computer monitor. The soundtrack grew louder still. The pentagram swung slower and slower until it was almost still. Mac's eyelids grew heavy. He closed them.

An ice-tipped spear lanced his heart.

Blackness enveloped him.

Chapter Seven

It was Kalfu's blackness—his dark side—that was beginning to frighten Magdeline Ortega. At one time, and it seemed not so long ago, she wouldn't have thought so. Her love spells, whether to return a straying lover, create attraction, or merely put the fire back into a waning relationship, were generally powerful and effective.

But lately, Kalfu, the master of the malevolent spirits of the night, the gatekeeper guarding the crossroads between the living and the dead, had become implacable, at least according to Maggie. Like a drug dealer offering enlightenment but serving up addiction, the powerful spirit was interfering with Legba, his twin occupying higher moral ground. Where Legba offered positive growth and change, true spiritual enlightenment, Kalfu was infamous for dragging his victims into lascivious pits of debauchery, oftentimes involving multiple prostitutes and crazy out-of-control drug and alcohol-laced orgies.

On the main drag of the tiny gated beach community called Costambar, Puerto Plata, Dominican Republic, Maggie had rented a small three-room office a few doors down from the popular supermarket, Yenny's. Three months to the day she had rented the space, creating a reception area, a bathroom, and another dimly lit room for love spells. The first month had been good, the second stellar, third stupendous. Foreigners, tired of the predatory money agenda of many Dominican and Haitian women, tired of fornicating with prostitutes, had begun consulting with her in droves.

They wanted what most people ultimately want—real, true love.

And, up until three days ago, she had a satisfied client base. But slowly it all started to unravel. At first it was little things. One client had complained that after his girlfriend had left his apartment for the evening, he had awoken the next day only to find himself in bed with a prostitute. He had no recollection of bringing her back to his apartment, let alone having sex with her. He knew he had a massive hangover, but didn't even remember drinking that much. Maggie had been able to explain that one away easily enough. Barry Fontaine was known by everyone in the community as a binge drinker, who suffered from blackouts. Double trouble. Lots of fun.

The second incident was a little more troubling. Maggie had cast a love spell on a woman Tom Springle had been courting for three months but with no success. Springle, in his 60s, was a teetotaler. At first the love spell had drawn Tom and Ingrid so close together they were almost joined at the hip. They were often seen necking and fondling in public, nothing really unusual around these parts.

After a few days of bliss, Tom woke up in a rented room of a Costambar brothel. Wouldn't have been so bad if he had been with his girlfriend Ingrid. Only problem was he was with five hookers, ten used condoms, and three empty forty-ounce bottles of rum. Again, Tom had no recollection of the event. He was lucky he was in a brothel, where the hookers were well-trained to be tight-lipped, at least where it concerned blabbing. So far, no word had spread to Ingrid. So far so good. Happy in love, true love, created by Maggie's powerful spell. Little damage control needed there.

But the third incident was the most troubling. It was the one that struck fear into Maggie's heart, fear of the dangerous and powerful spirit Kalfu. She sat at her desk and gazed out at the street. Motoconchos, motorcycle taxis, roared by. A few dogs barked. The hot afternoon sun was stifling, over a hundred degrees in the shade. Tourists ambled by, some staggering along bleary-eyed, zombie-like, swilling beer.

And then she saw him walk across the street. Michael Longhorn, the middle-aged American expat who had three years ago made Costambar his permanent home. He had called earlier and said, "I want to talk to you about that fucked up spell you put on me," and hung up the phone. He sounded angry and drunk. Maggie felt a bad vibe at the sound of his voice. She knew then, as she knew now, watching him approach, that something terrible had happened and maybe it was Kalfu's doing.

Wearing a white t-shirt and blue travel shorts, Michael entered the reception area, scratched the stubble on his pock-marked, sun-scorched face and sank into a chair facing Maggie. He looked at her with blue daggers, swilled a mouthful of beer, and set the bottle on the desk. The whites of his eyes were bloodshot.

Michael squeezed his fists and scowled at Maggie. "Do you know where I just came from?" He almost shouted the words.

"No," Maggie said, even though she did. "And would you mind keeping your voice down? We can deal with this like adults."

"Does that mean I get my thousand pesos back?" Michael barked, struggling to control his rising agitation.

"Listen Michael, I'm a fair and reasonable person. Why don't you explain to me exactly what happened. Maybe I can fix it."

"Oh, no," he said, raising a hand. "You tried to fix me last time and look what happened. Give me my money back. Your spells don't work. They aren't worth shit."

"Please calm down and tell me what happened."

Michael opened his mouth to speak and then all at once he looked deflated; overcome by emotional pain. He began to explain. At first the love spell Maggie had cast on he and Pamela Jimenez, a waitress at a beach bar and the object of his desire, had worked like a charm. Two days of bliss that felt like true love. But on the third day everything went south, or rather north into frigid temperatures.

After a romantic date with Pamela, Michael, who was not known as a big womanizer or a blackout drunk, had awoken early in the morning on Costambar beach, buck-naked with two naked women slumped on top of him and another two spread out beside him. A heap of used condoms and empty beer bottles were strewn all around. It was a policeman who had woken him, prodding him with a baton, like one would a cow with a branding iron. The cop politely informed Michael that one of the girls was under age—fifteen years old and two months pregnant. After much explaining, an afternoon in the Puerto Plata jail, and twenty thousand pesos, he was released. But of course news of the debacle had already spread to local newspapers, the local radio station, and gossip on the tiny beachfront community was rife. The result—Pamela stormed into his apartment this morning, angrily collected her few possessions, and told him, "Stay out of my life—forever."

Finishing the story, Michael's drunk blue eyes became sad. The anger had given way to sorrow, grief and heartache. "I love Pamela. I don't even remember hooking up with those other women. It's just not something I would do. I love her and what do I get—'Stay out of my life—forever.'"

Maggie brushed her long black hair aside, curled her hands together, and focused intense black eyes on Michael. Michael lowered his gaze and stared at the desk as if its pock-marked wooden surface contained the solutions to all his problems.

Cupid's arrow was finding its mark alright, but causing infidelity and breaking hearts everywhere. Maggie knew a refund wouldn't fix the problem. Word in the tiny community would spread like wild fire that her love spells were creating disastrous consequences. This had to be fixed, and fixed fast or her thriving little Voodoo love spell business would sink like a torpedo-impacted submarine.

Kalfu needed to be placated, satiated somehow or the powerful dark spirit would continue to wreak havoc on her love spells. A glass suddenly tipped over and a stream of water streaked across the desk, a fine line that snaked through papers, files and cell phones, without wetting them. She grabbed a paper towel, quickly wiping the water up, and lifting the glass.

Michael stared at the glass, pupils dilating. "I didn't touch the table."

"Neither did I." Maggie pointed to his beer bottle, which stood untouched. "And if you or I had, your bottle would have tipped over."

Michael looked at his half-full beer bottle, jerking his hand back, now too afraid to touch the lone soldier. "What the fuck just happened?" He stood up.

Maggie pointed to a tiny crack where the glass had previously been sitting. She didn't believe her words. "The glass was perched here, see. It's an uneven part of the table. It was probably ready to fall."

She knew damn well it was the work of angry spirits—Was Kalfu coming to get her?— but she also knew that was far too much information for Michael. She convinced him to sit down again.

After an initial protest, he did.

"Listen," she said, a spark igniting a tiny blaze of ideas in her head. "If you want your money back, I'll give it to you; although I'm not convinced what happened to you was a result of my magic. But I have a better idea."

"I'm listening. I would give my eye-teeth to get Pamela back."

Maggie explained another spell she had in mind, one she wanted to cast on Pamela and Michael. What she neglected to mention was there would be another unwilling participant. After five minutes of discussion, Michael agreed. She led him into a dimly lit room. They sat at a small table marked with an inverted pentagram, each point lit by a small flickering candle. Michael closed his eyes. Maggie held his hand and began chanting. A cold chill blew through the room and she shuddered, noticing goose bumps crawl up the arms of a now hypnotized Michael. A smile creased Maggie's pouty lips as she chanted and concocted. She knew if Mackenzie Adamson were aware of his role in the amended love spell, he would be terrified. And he would have every right to be.

But as the flickering flame in her mind exploded into an orange-red inferno of hellacious strategy, she was sure the new spell would be a win-win-win deal for everyone. And if it wasn't, well it was too late to worry about that now.

Chapter Eight

That was then. This is now, Mac thought, glancing into the mesmerizing chestnut-brown eyes of the object of his desire. Then, he couldn't even work up the courage or find the right moment to ask her for a date. Now, two days after Maggie had cast her spell and Christmas Eve to boot, he had just sat down to have a beer with her at a small table in a dimly lit corner of McNally's Pub.

The back-to-back blizzards had miraculously given way to clear skies, although it was still cold. The passable roads had allowed him a small window of opportunity that saw him drive into the gas station with a resolve he had never known. As if possessed by a divine intervention, he pulled up alongside Ophelia in the parking lot. As it turned out, she had just finished her shift and was heading home. Perfect timing.

As soon as he had parked beside her, she rolled down her window, offered a delightful smile and asked cheerily, "How are you?"

Mac exited his vehicle hastily, almost slipping on the icy pavement, and approached her car. The conversation played out almost exactly as it had in his mind a few days earlier. "Nice to see you Ophelia. I'm Mac by the way."

"Nice to see you again Mac."

"I don't have a lot of friends here and... well... it would be great if we could get together for a coffee or drink sometime. You know, just as friends."

Ophelia, the smile widening: "I'd like that."

Mac produced a business card and handed it to her. "Listen, here's my card, I'd really like it if you called me soon. We could make a plan and go out."

Ophelia took the business card, her smile turning to a small smirk. A smirk that promised devilishly sexy intentions. "I'll definitely call you. I'd love to go out. Have a great day now."

Replaying the conversation in his mind, Mac realized Ophelia was looking at him somewhat uncomfortably. He had sat down, started daydreaming, and had yet to speak a word to her. She was waiting patiently for the daydreaming to end, it seemed. He sipped his beer. "Sorry, sometimes I wander off into a world of my own."

"That's okay. I do that all the time. What were you daydreaming about anyway?"

Mac was about to offer a white lie, but instantly decided the truth was best. No point starting a relationship on the wrong foot. "I was thinking how great it would be to date you... and how the conversation to ask you out might unfold."

Ophelia sipped her beer, as her eyes darted around the near-empty bar. Maybe she was looking for the source of a new line of gossip that would surely spread like a blizzard through the tiny community. *Did you hear Mac and Ophelia are an item now? She's only twenty-five. Half his age. Can you imagine that*? Two patrons in a far corner played billiards and occasionally glanced over at their table. The female bartender and male owner sat at the bar engaged in conversation, likely shop-talk. Multiple television screens broadcast sporting events, mostly hockey games. Outside, the sky was black, the moon was full, with millions of twinkling stars accentuating its glow. Finally, Ophelia spoke: "And did it unfold like you thought?"

"As a matter of fact it did." Mac said, fighting but failing to control a slight blush that spread across his cheeks. He hoped it was dark enough that Ophelia wouldn't notice. "I have to admit, I've had a crush on you for a long time, from the minute I saw you really." *So much for the dating-as-friends line. You don't even know if she has a boyfriend.*

Ophelia returned the blush and smiled. "I kind of liked you when I first saw you too. And, no I don't have a boyfriend, if that's what you're wondering. Do you have a girlfriend?"

Mac shook his head. "I've been so busy renovating I didn't have time for that. Besides, it seems to me there isn't exactly an abundance of women around here. Maybe in Charlottetown but it's a bit of a commute for me."

Ophelia nodded. Then she changed the subject. "What are you doing for Christmas?"

In his excitement about the date, the fog created by the depression demons, and the culture shock of transitioning to the Island, not to mention the nasty storms of late, and the mouse invasion, Mac had completely forgotten that today was December 24th. At that thought he was even more wowed by Ophelia agreeing to have a drink with him on Christmas Eve. Shouldn't she be with family? Maybe they celebrated the holiday tomorrow, as many Canadians did. "I don't have any plans yet. I don't have many friends and no family here. You?"

"Not much." Ophelia Sallis explained she was an only child, rented a small apartment in Montague, and her mother Elaine lived a few blocks away in a rented apartment. She was estranged from her father Tyrone who had left Elaine two years ago for a younger woman and had moved to Calgary where the money was. Ophelia had taken sides with her mother and hadn't spoken to her father since the split. All she had planned was to meet her mother on Christmas day to have dinner—lasagna instead of the traditional turkey. Just the two of them sharing quality time, the exchange of one gift each and a meal in a small two-bedroom apartment. Nothing fancy.

As she talked, Ophelia's eyes focused intently on his. Finishing the story, she suddenly touched his hand. Her palm was like warm velvet and Mac couldn't help the stirrings of desire.

"Why don't we have our own Christmas this evening?" she suggested, a mischievous smile playing across her lips.

Mac looked at her, awestruck. It was happening. The woman of his dreams was suggesting a Christmas of their own, just the two of them, and the twinkle in her eyes hinted at a lot more. For a moment, Mac couldn't speak. He opened his mouth but no words came out.

"Are you okay?"

Ophelia glided her sensuous fingertips along his forearm and removed her hand slowly.

Goosebumps crawled up his arms. "Uh... I'm sorry... I can't believe you just said that."

She stood up and extended a hand. "I said it. Let's go. The grocery store closes in an hour."

******

Two hours later they were cuddled up in Mac's queen-sized bed, fully clothed, listening to Christmas Carols on the radio. Ophelia had dropped her car off at her apartment and climbed into Mac's pick-up. They stopped at the grocery store, purchased a prepared salad, a cooked barbeque-flavored chicken, and a loaf of Italian bread. Leaving town, they also stopped at the liquor store and bought a 26-ounce bottle of rum, three bottles of Chilean red wine and a 24-pack of beer.

During a candlelit dinner, in the peacefulness and tranquility unique to the Island, they dined, drank wine and chatted. Mac told her about his background, omitting the parts about the recent depression, nightmares, botched relationships and especially Maggie's spell. A little at a time is always best. No point in spilling his guts on the first date. She'd probably think he was some kind of a nutcase.

For her part, she talked only briefly about one long-term relationship she had with a man of her age, who every winter went west to the oilfields of Alberta to work. There was no real acrimony in the relationship, she explained. It was just she couldn't handle the long absences without his company, so decided to break it off. She knew it would be difficult to find a man of her age on the Island who would be around permanently; after all, the money was west of the Island, but she had convinced herself it was for the best. Ophelia didn't want an absentee boyfriend. Although independent enough, she planned on attending veterinary school next September and she wanted a serious relationship and a family of at least two children. Fortunately for Mac, their age difference wasn't an issue.

"Age is just a number in your head," she said, flicking away an unruly lock of curly blonde hair. "You're as young as you feel. And you look young for your age."

As he cuddled beside her, Mac thought about the comment, realizing that indeed she was right. To onlookers, the age difference probably wouldn't be that apparent. At least she didn't look like his daughter, like some of the made-in-the-Dominican-Republic relationships Mac had seen. Crotchety wrinkled old men with beer bellies walking around with nineteen-year-old women. Did they really think the women loved them for them, or did it even matter to them anymore? Maybe at their age bought love with the woman of their dreams was better than no love at all. Besides, in the Dominican Republic it costs a hell of a lot less to keep a beautiful young woman around than in Canada, or the United States for that matter. Mac didn't have the answers, probably never would. But he did know the woman beside him now, staring up at the ceiling idly, was certainly the woman of his dreams. Was it possible he could keep her?

She turned over, traced an index finger down his cheek and across his lips. "What are you thinking, Mac?"

He snuggled in close and slowly moved in for the first kiss. "This is the best Christmas I've ever had."

They kissed, a peck at first, but then a second one, longer, and a third, longer still and more passionate. Ophelia glided her tongue along Mac's lips. He thought it was the best sensation he had felt in his entire life. It was more than that. It was electrifying. Finally the kiss ended. She withdrew a few inches and locked eyes with his.

"Ditto," she said.

Mac leaned over, lifted a glass of wine from the candlelit bedside table, handed it to Ophelia and reached for his own.

She smiled.

He smiled. "Cheers. May the spirit of the crossroads keep us happy together."

As soon as he said it, Mac wasn't sure exactly what he had meant. Somehow, the words had escaped his lips devoid of conscious thought.

Ophelia, too, looked baffled. "What does that mean?"

"I don't know," Mac said, wrinkling his brow. "But Merry Christmas to you. And thanks so much for keeping me company tonight."

They clinked glasses, drank, set them down, and got lost in a passionate embrace of kissing—freely and eagerly letting their hands wander.

"Ohh, Ophelia," Mac said, getting lost in the intense pleasure of the moment. "You turn me on so much. You're so beautiful. It feels so good... sooo good... you make me crazy."

"Ohh," Ophelia moaned as Mac glided inside her. "Ohh, don't stop... like that... that's it... like that... ohh, ohh, ohh... Don't stop..."

Chapter Nine

"Stop, stop, you're hurting me," she said.

Wiping a sweaty brow, Mac stopped thrusting.

He eyed the woman lying on the bed and realized, cold terror icing his veins, she wasn't Ophelia. Her blue eyes welled with tears. A bedside lamp illuminated long black hair matted to the side of her sweat-soaked face. Her full lips formed a grimace. Adrenaline surging through his body, he darted his eyes quickly around the room, realizing in an instant he was not in his house. It was a hotel suite. The blinds were pulled shut. It was dark.

He quickly pulled out of the distraught woman and climbed out of bed. A dull throbbing pain pounded in his head—a hangover headache. He scanned the floor, noticing a crumpled mass of clothing, his and hers. Used condoms and empty beer cans cluttered the plush red carpet.

She pulled the blanket up, covering her small pear-shaped breasts. Her grimace turned to a frown. "It was good. But I'm not a machine, you know. I already came six times to your four. I'm sore."

"Who are you?" Mac said with rising panic. His tone bordered on hysterical. He scooped up his underwear and pulled them on, over his condom-wrapped erect member.

"I'm Jalisa. Don't you remember?"

"No."

Mac scooped up the remainder of his clothing, hurried into the bathroom, and closed the door.

"We met downtown on Queen Street. You invited me here," she said. "You said you'd pay me. I hope you're not planning on ripping me off."

Inside the bathroom, Mac removed the condom and tossed it in the wastebasket. His throbbing member protested, wanting more. As he dressed, thoughts tumbled through his mind like an avalanche. *Jalisa? Queen Street? I'm in Charlottetown. How did I get here? I said I'd pay her? What happened to Ophelia? What day is it? What the fuck is going on here?*

Jalisa's voice, slightly irritated, from behind the door: "You are going to pay me aren't you?"

"Yes... don't worry I'll pay."

Mac wanted the problem to go away, and he wanted the hell out of whatever hotel he was in. He had drawn a blackout the size of a crater on the moon and had no idea of the possible consequences. He finished dressing, splashed some cold water on his face, towel-dried it, and glanced in the mirror. Bloodshot green eyes with dilated pupils and dark circles under them. His hazy gaze was far from lucid. Not good. Not good at all.

He emerged from the bathroom, absently running a hand across his forehead. The dull throbbing pain was intensifying. Frowning, he realized the big head was throbbing in perfect timing with the mission-driven little head. *Not tonight dear I have a headache. How about, okay tonight dear, I have a headache in both heads and it's the only way to relieve the pain? The throbbing pain. Stop it... get your shit together and get out of here.*

Wrapped in a towel, standing and holding her clothes, Jalisa said, "Are you okay? You look out of it."

With rising fear, Mac realized he had retreated inside a head he felt he was losing control of. *You're losing control of both heads, buddy.* He wiped his eyes. "What day is it?"

Walking past him into the bathroom, Jalisa cast a sideways puzzled glance and rolled her eyes. "It's boxing day silly. We spent Christmas together. Don't you remember?"

Mac stared at her blankly. She closed the bathroom door behind her. He continued eyeing the white bathroom door for a long while until he heard the shower running. He hurriedly gathered his belongings, which amounted to a winter jacket, money and credit cards in a plastic pocket-sized insurance folder, a black Budweiser baseball cap, a pair of gloves and some winter boots.

After a second search, he found his smart phone in the drawer of a bedside table. He checked the time. 8:46 pm. Fuck. He had lost almost two days. He quickly thumbed through the call log, noticing two missed calls, two voice-mails and two text messages. The text messages were from Ophelia. So, it was true. He had made contact with her. And the last thing he remembered was... making love to her on Christmas Eve... was that also true or had he imagined the whole thing, replacing Jalisa in his mind's eye with Ophelia?

He read Ophelia's text messages: *Mac, we need to talk.* And the second one: *Mac, you're in deep shit. Call me when you get this.*

Mac's heart skipped a beat. Cold terror raced through his body almost freezing him to the spot. *What the fuck have I done?* After a few seconds of paralysis, he forced his unwilling legs to move to the bedroom window, absently pulling the blinds open and looking out. Through blizzard-whipped winds, faint headlights illuminated Grafton Street as cars drove through the snowstorm. Through a blanket of falling snow, he could barely make out the name of the hotel on the neon sign: *Maritime Inn.*

He swallowed a lump of fear and forced it into the pit of a stomach that had begun to churn uncomfortably. He picked up a glass of water from the bedside table and choked it back, wiping away a stream of dribble that snaked down his chin, neck and shirt.

He fought the urge to vomit. After a minute, it subsided. He cleaned up the room, picking up beer cans and placing them on a mirrored vanity. He deposited the condoms and wrappers in a wastebasket. He tucked the phone in his jeans, putting on the winter jacket, boots and baseball cap.

Fully dressed in tight-fitting blue jeans and a white pullover top, Jalisa emerged from the bathroom, combing her thick long hair. She stood about five-foot-two.

Beautiful, Mac thought. *Like a smaller version of Salma Hayek. Forget the beauty, you idiot. Pay her, get the fuck out of here and call Ophelia.* "I... we have to go. How much do I owe you?"

"Don't you remember? I could tell you anything and you'd pay it. What... you got a wife waiting at home or something? Maybe a possessive girlfriend?"

"Please. I don't want any problems."

"You're lucky I'm honest. We agreed on four hundred a night... let's see, Christmas Eve, Christmas day and today, Boxing Day. That's three nights—you owe me twelve hundred."

"But you didn't spend the night tonight?" *Christmas Eve? Was it her and not Ophelia I made love to on Christmas Eve? Don't argue money you fool. Pay her and leave.*

"Doesn't matter. If you negotiate a nightly rate and send me home early, that's your problem. You negotiated an overnight rate, not an hourly rate. There's a difference you know."

Mac fished a wad of one hundred dollar bills from his pocket. Evidently, he had even gone to the bank and withdrawn money in preparation for the sexcapade. Things were getting stranger—and scarier—by the second. He peeled off twelve hundred dollar bills and handed them to Jalisa, shuddering when he realized things could have turned out a lot worse. *You're not out of here yet, bro. Don't count your chickens.*

"Thanks," she said, gathering up what little belongings she had there. She picked up her black purse, stuffed some toiletries inside, and approached the door, which Mac was nervously holding open. She pursed her lips. "Don't I get a kiss? At least if you're going to fuck me you can kiss me you know."

Mac gave her a quick peck on the lips.

Leaving the room, she grinned. "You got my number, right?"

Mac nodded. He had no idea if he did.

"Then call me sometime. I'd like to do this again... but please, not so fast, furious and often next time. You're a fucking tiger in bed. El tigre!"

******

Thirty-three minutes later, Mac had paid the hotel bill to the young male hotel clerk, with the knowing smirk, and dropped Jalisa off at a small brick two-storey house on a quiet street in downtown Charlottetown. Slowly and nervously, he navigated blizzard-blown roads on his way home. He had just heard a radio disc jockey call the back-to-back storms and deep-freeze temperatures a polar vortex, an extreme weather event affecting parts of Canada, the United States—as far south as central Florida—and even Northeastern Mexico.

As he pulled over into the parking lot of a highway gas station, he felt like he too had been sucked into some sort of sexual vortex, drawing him into a life of lasciviousness and debauchery. It was far from his normal modus operandi to pursue a woman he had a big-time crush on only to wander off the same night and negotiate a deal with a hooker in downtown Charlottetown *and fuck her like a tiger*. As he pulled into a parking stall, extracted his phone and began to dial Ophelia, he wondered what else he might have done—that he couldn't remember—during the hours from Christmas Eve to Boxing Day evening. He shuddered to think he could've even done something criminal like kill someone and have absolutely no recollection of it.

As the phone rang, it came to him in an instant: something had gone terribly wrong with Maggie's love spell. He had to contact her to try and reverse the effects before something really insane occurred, if it already hadn't.

Ophelia picked up on the third ring. "Mac, we need to talk. Where were you?"

Even though he was sitting down, he had to think on his feet. "I was... I was in Charlottetown, spending Christmas with a friend. I forgot my phone at home." He realized as soon as he said it how stupid it sounded, but he had to say something. He was only halfway home. What if she asked where he was now?

"Where are you now?"

"I'm just getting some coffee at the Esso in Murray River. Then I'm heading home," he said, rapidly trying to invent a friend in Charlottetown should she ask who he was with.

Maybe she didn't know him well enough to start asking about the nature of his other relationships. *Didn't I say I have no friends?* Mac couldn't remember. But she didn't ask. Thank God. He didn't want to start a relationship, piling lie on top of lie on top of lie, building a mountain of lies that would one day crack, creak, groan and bury him neck-deep in a landslide of deception.

Instead, she said, "Okay. Call me when you get home, okay?"

"I will." After a moment's pause. "I had a great time with you last night... I mean Christmas Eve."

There was a deafening silence on the other end of the line that seemed to last for minutes. It was actually two seconds. "That's what I wanted to talk to you about," Ophelia said.

They said their goodbyes, and Mac pulled back onto the highway. He had planned on grabbing a coffee at the service station but had forgotten all about it. Ophelia's tone had a note of urgency that said get home now and call me—this is something very important.

What did I do to her that night? By the time Mac had pulled into his driveway, twice almost spinning the Dodge into a ditch while sliding on icy roads, his swerving brain had invented multiple scenarios: *I hit her. I beat her. I didn't even make love with her. I imagined the whole thing. It was Jalisa the whole time. I said something to offend her. I yelled at her. I disrespected her.*

And by the time he entered his house, both his hands were shaking near-uncontrollably and the pounding in his head had escalated to sledgehammer force. Before he called Ophelia, he had another call to make. He had to reach Maggie and find out what the fuck had gone wrong with her love spell—find a way to change it before Ophelia labelled him a psycho and decided to stay as far away from him as the confines of the tiny Island would allow.

Chapter Ten

There were few things she would allow. And deception was not one of them. It didn't matter to forty-six-year-old Livia Johnson that she was the master of deception, a master at luring foreigners—vacationers or permanent residents—into her clutches, seducing them with her ample bosom, sculpted body, attractive face and multiple charms. It was all right for her to do the deceiving, but not okay for the male victims of her seductive charms to play at that game. In her world, it didn't take two to tango—it only took one, and she was it.

Her game, perfected over the last five years, had been distilled to its simple essence. Lure a foreigner with money, make him fall in love with her, milk him for all he was worth—figuratively and literally—and then dump him on the beach like so many Dominicans do with their unwanted trash.

Although Livia had multiple sexual partners, it wasn't all right for the man she called her boyfriend to conduct his life in Costambar in the same fashion. Once it was declared they were an item, he was hers and hers only to do with and dispose of as she chose.

And as she sat at a table in Pasqual's beach bar that sunny afternoon, watching the chiseled bare-chested handsome man stroll along the beach, she wondered if he had the capacity for deception. She had been watching him for three days now, stalking him really. He hung around in the three most popular beach bars of Costambar. She had seen Brad Simonson on two occasions meet with Dominican hookers but had never seen him flaunt them in public. She knew them by name and reputation. Good, reliable hookers that went reasonably cheaply and wouldn't steal from you, upcharge you, or start playing the love-money game with you. They serviced you, took their payment and left. Brad had picked well on his first week in Costambar. And she had also learned the unsuspecting American from New York was a wealthy airline pilot who had his sights set on buying a condo in the beachfront community and living at least eight months of the year here.

A perfect mark.

But it was the recent conflicting information that bothered Livia as she watched Brad stop, gaze out at the ocean and clear blue sky for a moment, and then resume strolling. A friend had told her he was single, another that he had a wife and was lying about being single. Maybe he was out to take advantage of unsuspecting women. He had already fucked at least two hookers, so he did enjoy sex. That was a good thing, Livia thought, still following him with her intent gaze. But, it wouldn't be so good if he had a wife, who might show up any moment and ruin Livia's plans. That wouldn't be good at all. For her plan to work letter-perfect, her victim had to be single. She didn't live in a posh 1,200 square-foot beachside condo for nothing. She lived in it—and owned it outright—because she had been very calculating and intelligent with her efforts. And she wasn't about to have her game ruined by a man, least of all by someone with less brains than herself.

Aren't they all stupider than me? she thought, as she sipped her beer. Maybe Brad did harbor the capacity for deception; maybe he would even try and hold a candle to her mastery of the virtue—yes, to Livia it was a virtue—but she had to find out. Find out if he had a wife, find out if he had the capacity to beat her at her own game, find out if he could be played—like so many others before him—like a well-tuned guitar. But to find out, she had to initiate phase one of her plan—a phase she had affectionately coined the Attraction Phase.

She grinned, licked her lips, swallowed a mouthful of beer (she would be swallowing a lot more than that soon) rose, flicked off her white cotton camisole, and jogged toward the ocean, ostensibly to go for a dip. A few restaurant patrons ogled Livia's bouncing bikini-clad bosom and tight buttocks.

A few more grinned and nodded, some arching eyebrows. They had seen the charade before. They knew and didn't care.

She approached Brad, who walked close to the water's edge. A few feet in front of his path, she tripped and fell flat on her face in the sand, some granules splashing up her nose and into her eyes. A little sand in the face was worth it, she thought, as she grimaced in mock-pain, grabbed her ankle, and watched the look of concern on Brad's face as he rushed to her aid.

He knelt down beside her.

"Are you okay?" His handsome features were tight with genuine concern.

"I... I think I sprained my ankle. Could you help me up please?"

"Of course," he said, pointing. "Here... let's get you to a chair."

Brad helped her up slowly and, enveloping her with muscular arms, led her limping gingerly to a waiting table at Pasqual's.

"I don't think I know you," Livia said as he helped her to a plastic chair. "I'm Livia. Livia Johnson."

"Brad."

He shook her hand. "I've seen you around, but we've never met."

Livia held his hand a little longer than Canadian cultural norms permitted. She loosened her grip and gently caressed his palm, smiling and revealing perfect white teeth.

Brad returned the smile.

A waitress, with a knowing look and a plastic bag of ice, approached. She handed the bag to Brad and he knelt down and pressed it to the ankle. Only two hours ago, she had rubbed it red in her apartment, anticipating the game, knowing the mark.

Brad pushed an empty chair in front of her leg and pointed to it. "You should elevate it and put the ice on."

Livia smiled. "Good idea… could you help me?"

Brad knelt down, carefully lifted her leg and stretched it out on the chair. He gently placed the bag of ice on the "affected ankle."

"Thanks so much," Livia said, beaming. "Can I buy you a drink?"

Brad nodded. "I'd love a beer… but I'll pay."

"Are you sure?"

"Of course. Beer is cheap here."

"Okay. But I insist I get the next one."

"I won't argue if you insist."

"That's a good boy."

As they talked, about the weather and how great it was not to be in Vancouver, where Livia was from, how great it was for Brad not to be in New York, which was currently getting pounded by ferocious storms, and just how great it was to sit on the beach in paradise mid-afternoon and drink beer and stare out at the deep blue sea, a plot was hatching in Livia's mind—a plot that would see Brad regret the day he ever met her, regret the day he was ever born.

As Livia had.

Growing up in a rich household in Vancouver, she was the youngest of three sisters, all of whom had managed to find love and marry successfully. Tammy and Bonnie were also successful in their own right. Tammy was a talented writer who had just recently hit the bestseller list with one of her romance novels. Bonnie also had a flair for the craft, but concentrated her efforts on writing killer ad-copy for a prestigious downtown advertising firm. Livia, on the other hand, couldn't hold down a job, or a relationship. She had become jealous of her sister's successes, more jealous that her parents—married for twenty-five years—still had a spark in their successful relationship. She had often asked, "Why should they have what I can't?" Or, "Why was I born this way?"

Those questions had led her down this current path. And how it manifested itself was that men should pay for her sadness. One of her first relationships in Vancouver was with Bruce Stripton. Three months into it, he called her a "possessive psycho who couldn't hold down a monogamous relationship if your life depended on it," and walked out the door, never to return.

Then there was Steve Batterfry.

Two months in, he said, "I see a money agenda here and a propensity for promiscuity." He slammed the door in her face and never looked back.

Livia had vowed revenge on those men, but never exacted it. And she had even started to recover somewhat by the time the third man came along. But the third man turned into the third strike—strike three and you're out—and that changed her permanently and irrevocably. It gave her pause to reflect on her modus operandi and perfect it. If the marks realized something was up, usually by then it was too late and it wouldn't matter. She would be done with them, and have her clutches in at least a sizable portion of their wealth. And they would be left to suffer emotionally and financially.

Brad droned on about his life as a pilot. Livia only half-listened but smiled and laughed and threw in her two cents at all the appropriate times. He would be an easy target. But her mind was elsewhere.

Thinking about the third strike, she wondered if she had the propensity for murder. She had broken the arm of one of her victims with a well-placed kick, pummeled another repeatedly in the face while shit-faced, attacked another one with a butcher knife (the target had been a big man who had easily disarmed her). What would she do with the third strike? His rejection had changed her forever and had solidified her purpose—to degrade and use the male species.

She replayed the conversation in her mind, the hurtful things he had said when he dumped her just over four years ago in Vancouver:

"... I don't ever want to see you again. Lose my fucking phone number. Hell, you've got plenty of others anyway... fuck you... you fucking bitch."

Livia frowned, only slightly, as she remembered her last screaming, pain-filled reply: *"YOU'RE A FUCKING ASSHOLE AND I WILL SEE YOU GET YOUR COMEUPPANCE!!"*

But then the frown transformed to a smile when she remembered the man would soon be arriving in Puerto Plata. She would dispense with Brad in short order and exact her revenge on the one she blamed for all her problems, the man who was responsible for her inability to find true love—the third strike.

Oh yes, she thought, arching a brow and grinning. Mackenzie Adamson would pay dearly for his indignities.

Chapter Eleven

A week later, Mackenzie Adamson pressed pay on the West jet website and sighed, realizing, for better or worse, he would be flying into Puerto Plata tomorrow, January 3, 2014, to meet with Voodoo witch Maggie to try and reverse the nasty side effects of her botched love spell. While being evasive with the details, Maggie had admitted during a Skype conversation that something had gone wrong and the only way to repair it was for Mac to meet with her in person. So he had agreed. Not like he had a choice after the nasty news of late.

Things had gotten worse since he arrived home that Boxing Day evening after the unremembered episode with Jalisa Evans. He had had another short phone conversation with Ophelia in which her tone sounded distant and cold. She had something to say to Mac and she wanted to say it in person, not over the phone. So they met the following afternoon in Tim Horton's coffee shop in Montague; she insisted she wanted to meet in public rather than in private, and Ophelia spilled her guts, if that's what you wanted to call it.

First there was the Christmas Eve party at Mac's house. She said everything had been going well until they started making love. During the session, which had started off hot, passionate and gentle, Mac's dark green eyes turned zombie-like and frightened her. His emotionless eyes weren't looking at her. They were penetrating her, as if there was some yet-to-be-realized debauchery lying in wait, an insatiable appetite for more, more, more sex. And then his gentle caressing became rough and passionless.

And the things he said: "Take it you bitch... fuck me hard... ride my fucking cock like you love it." And one line which particularly offended her: "Fuck me to death, you fucking slut."

Mac had listened to Ophelia with downcast eyes, barely able to make eye contact. He saw the hurt, saw the pain, saw her eyes well up with tears and felt helpless to comfort her. What could he say? He had done those things, said those things, even though he didn't remember any of it. He knew on some gut level it wasn't him acting out; it was someone, something else, far more powerful and evil. And although he realized everything that had happened had to do with Maggie's spell, he had been unable to tell Ophelia. What would she make of such a harebrained excuse? Who would believe his behavior was a botched love spell? So he had hung his head and taken the lecture like a scorned school boy.

According to Ophelia, after their lovemaking session, he had left the bed quickly, without any post-coital cuddle, dressed hurriedly, opened the door and said, "I think we're done for the night."

Then he ushered her out the door and drove her home, barely saying a word.

That would have been enough, should have been enough. But there had been more. Rumors had started to circulate around town—some true, some twisted into part truth part fiction, the result of being churned through the rumor mill and spit out like some mutant aberration. Sometime between Christmas Eve and Boxing Day, Mac had apparently made a few trips to Montague, approached at least a half-dozen women in public and rather inappropriately asked them out on dates. On one occasion, he'd even smacked a young woman's tight little ass and told her, "That would look much better with my cock in it."

Ophelia said the distraught and offended woman was considering pressing charges for sexual assault.

Finishing the story, eyes welling with tears, Ophelia had lifted Mac's downcast face so he could see the pain in her eyes, and said: "Mac, you have a serious problem. Everyone thinks you're some kind of a sick sexual predator, maybe even a pedophile or a rapist. I can't have a relationship with someone like that."

She had stood up, turned around, and stormed out of the coffee shop while other patrons murmured and cast disapproving glances at Mac. Mac had been sure one scowling behemoth of a man was going to attack and pound him into Jello. It had been all he could do to quickly leave the coffee shop, get into his vehicle, and high-tail it out of there.

During the last few days, other than getting on top of the mouse problem, his situation had not improved. The exterminators had come in, sprayed, set up more poison bait stations and pointed out the problem areas to Mac: a few holes in the basement foundation he had missed. The basement had been literally crawling with mice ever since Old Man Winter swept in with snow and bitter cold. So Mac had sealed the holes, and sealed himself in the house for the last five days (*Fuck New Year's Day, I've got jack-shit to celebrate*), even going so far as to padlock both doors from the inside, hide the keys in a plastic bag in the toilet bowl tank, and hope and pray that another blackout didn't occur.

And as far as he knew, he hadn't blacked out, left the house and committed any assaults of any kind. Each morning he would dutifully check to insure the padlocks were in place, breathe a sigh of relief when he realized they were, and go about planning the trip to Puerto Plata. The black demons of depression had been replaced by black demons of fear, and one part of Mac wished for the simple and uncomplicated life he once had. At least the depression had been manageable. But this fear, this horrific realization that he was not himself anymore and could be capable of murder, sexual assault, maybe even full-blown rape, was driving him out of his mind. At the very slightest creak and groan of the old house, his flesh would crawl with goose bumps, he would break into a cold sweat, his throat would parch and his heart would rattle in its cage like a rabid rat.

The nights were the worst. He would toss and turn and break into hot and cold sweats while trying to sleep. It was the images that drove him mad, preventing deep sleep from taking root. Orgiastic frenzies—some Mac would observe, others he would participate in—laced with alcohol, more positions than the Kama Sutra and hundreds of grinning, laughing, moaning naked female forms. And when the images would fade, the feverish sweats begin to break, then the devilish, haunting face would materialize. It was a face, not unlike the Joker in Batman, but yet very distinct in and of itself. A black top hat sat above chiseled features, blood-red skin, a forked serpent tongue, eye slits with jet-black pupils and white fangs. As the evil monster would fade and Mac would pull himself tight into a fetal position, waiting for the powerful sleeping pills to take effect, the heckling, cawing laughter would start. It would be high-pitched and loud for a few mind-rattling minutes, and slowly fade into nothing. That's when a thin restless sleep would finally envelop Mac for a few hours, only for him to wake again to relieve himself; a cold chill permeating his body and a sense of impending doom numbing his precariously balanced senses. He would return to bed and have the whole horrible experience start all over again—until drug-induced sleep (with dosages getting dangerously higher by the day) would finally intervene and drag him into the black hole of nothingness.

And that was only the half of it. The nightmares were often much worse than the orgy-infested-cackling-monster precursor to more dark terror. Through his haze, Mac started to notice a theme to the nightmares, many of which he would remember vividly upon waking. The theme was simple. They all involved rum. Some involved guns and all involved beautiful women. There would be a beautiful Dominican or Haitian woman who would approach him, perhaps on the beach in Costambar. She would seduce him with her physical attributes, maybe a witty Spanish phrase or seductive smile. Mac would negotiate a price and take her home to his penthouse apartment for rum—Cuba libre was his drink of choice—and sex. The sex would be wild and satisfying, but the end wouldn't be so pleasant; troubling things. Mac would notice money missing, once even a cell phone disappeared. One time all the apartment neighbors leered over their balconies and heckled while watching a hooker leave Mac's apartment. Sometimes a terror-filled struggle would occur and Mac would have great difficulty getting the woman to leave. In one nightmare, a Haitian woman drunk out of her black curly-haired skull, turned loud, obnoxious and violent. Her screaming temper tantrum woke neighbors. Eventually the cops arrived, hauled

Mac off to prison, and told him he would be doing a long time in jail after they convicted him of rape. In another, a Dominican man entered the apartment as a woman was leaving, sliced Mac to pieces with a machete, robbed the apartment and vanished. Yet another post-sex terror: two men entered with guns and riddled Mac with bullets. And another: a hooker went ballistic, trashing Mac's apartment and smashing him over the head with a coffee-maker before fleeing the apartment with his money and valuables.

And there were more, but Mac didn't want to think about the details right now. They were beginning to terrify him. But he couldn't help wondering if they were premonition dreams. Would all this terror be realized when he landed in Puerto Plata?

He printed his plane ticket, rubbed tired eyes entombed in hollow black sockets, and glanced at the clock: 2:33 pm. And he felt it—the mid-day fatigue, side effects from sleeping pills that he was rapidly becoming addicted to. But he fought the urge to sleep. Fought it because he knew knowledge was power. But, in his case, he felt it was much more than power. Knowledge was life. His life. If he had any chance at all of escaping this evil curse, he was convinced was now possessing him, the first thing he had to do was learn about it. He must learn as much about his enemy as he could. He began frantically searching the internet to find the enemy's name.

After thirty minutes of reading about Haitian Voodoo, Mac was sure he had found it: Kalfu, the spirit of the crossroads, was often envisioned as a young man or as a demon. Red in color—like Mac's visions—he likes rum infused with gunpowder and is often, if not mistakenly, recognized as the spirit of the night, associated with sexual debauchery, bad luck, deliberate destruction, misfortune and injustices.

Mac became engrossed—and more frightened—reading about Kalfu's good and bad deeds.

He almost jumped out of his skin when he heard a loud metallic rapping at his back door. He stood quickly, swinging his arms wildly and almost knocking over a desk lamp. He peeked down the hallway and frowned, forcing the ball of fear down into his stomach and willing his pounding heart to slow.

Two cops stood at the door, peering through the window curiously.

"I'll be right there," Mac said, hurrying to the door.

He went into the bathroom, fished the keys out of the toilet tank, fumbled with the lock for a few seconds, and finally opened the door.

The mid-afternoon wind howled and hissed.

The officers introduced themselves as Detective Byron Casey and Detective Roy Banner. Banner, a red-mustached man with a large beer belly, said, "Is there a reason you're locking yourself in your house?"

Mac stared blankly at the cop for a few seconds while Casey, a thinner and taller man with clean-cut features and slicked-back black hair, grinned.

"I sleep-walk sometimes. I found myself in the middle of a snowdrift one night."

Mac felt his hands beginning to twitch with nervousness—*Did I kill someone?* He clasped them together in an effort to stop them from shaking.

Banner studied Mac's still quivering hands.

"Do you sleep-walk at 2:30 in the afternoon?" Casey asked, his mouth widening to something resembling a shit-eating smirk.

"I do if I take an afternoon nap," Mac lied. "And I was just about to do that... tell me detectives, what is the purpose of your visit?"

Even though it was cold and windy outside, Mac wasn't about to let the cops in for fear they would overstay their welcome, bait him into a trap, and before he knew it he would be arrested for something and taken into custody. He had to leave the country. And fast.

"Listen," Banner said with a scowl. "We've heard some nasty rumors about your behavior around town lately. We know you're new to the Island and I'm going to tell you straight out right now... we don't tolerate any bullshit around here. You..."

"I don't know what you're talking about," Mac said, feeling his cheeks flush.

"I think you know exactly what I'm talking about," Banner said. "You're walking around like a fucking pervert, asking anyone with a pair of tits out on a date. I hear you're touching them inappropriately."

Banner stepped forward, moving his grizzled face to within a few inches from Mac's.

Mac stepped back and closed the door a few inches. Banner grabbed the door, jerking it open roughly, and stuffed his head inside, about six inches from Mac's face. Mac smelled acrid tobacco breath.

"Listen you little shit," Banner said. "I don't know much about you yet, but what I do know isn't very charming. If I hear another word from any of the women around town, I'm going to arrest your ass so fast you won't be able to say Jackrabbit."

Jackrabbit, Jackrabbit, stick a Jackrabbit up your ass, Mac thought, but bit his tongue, not quite fast enough to conceal a smirk.

"You think it's funny?" Banner asked, pushing the screen door open so forcefully it crashed into Mac's arm and pushed him back a step.

"I didn't invite you into my house, and unless you have a warrant for my arrest you can fuck right off."

Surprised by his own words, but none-the-less pleased by his new-found bravado, Mac fought once again unsuccessfully to wipe the smirk off his face. He was changing indeed. This marked the first time he had ever cursed at two officers of the law. He knew if he tried this approach in the Dominican Republic he would likely be shot, get the living shit kicked out of him, or wind up in a squalid jail for a very long time. Or all of the above.

Casey's grin had miraculously transformed into an angry scowl. He stepped forward.

But the words seemed to have surprised Banner, who stepped back, just long enough for Mac to slam the screen door shut in his face and lock it.

Mac examined the scratch on his arm, the result of the screen door's impact. He rolled with the new-found bravado, mixed with a tinge of anger. "Unless you have a warrant, I don't want to see you on my property again."

More foul language formed on the tip of Mac's tongue but he managed to swallow it and offer a slightly more diplomatic and polite farewell. "Now would you two mind getting on your high horses and riding off into the sunset. I have a nap to take. And you're interfering with my schedule."

Banner's face contorted into something resembling, at least to Mac, a hissing snake. He opened his mouth to speak but Casey grabbed his arm and shot him a look. Its meaning was not missed on Mac. Bide your time, my brother, we'll get him later.

Mac watched the cops step off the porch and walk to their black unmarked Crown Vic. Banner opened the driver's door and covered his eyes as a strong gust of wind dusted him with powdery snow. Then, the angry scowl returned.

"Disrespect the law, will you?" Banner waved an index finger, like a mother scolding an unruly child. "The next time we see you you'll wish you were never born."

Mac knew he had gone too far, but yet some powerful, eerie and uncontrollable force pushed him on. He unlocked the screen door, poked his head out and, grinning widely, said, "Have your selves a very nice day gentlemen. Next time I'll have coffee and donuts ready."

He punctuated his words by slamming the screen door shut with such force that he almost slipped and fell on his ass.

Chapter Twelve

"Oh you made an ass out of yourself last night. You just don't remember," Ryan Jones, a Canadian who spent his winters in Costambar, said.

"I did?" Mac asked, wearily regarding the other eyes around the table.

Mid-afternoon; he was sitting with six other foreigners in beachfront restaurant and bar, El Carey. Thirty feet away, fierce waves pounded the shoreline. High winds whipped and dark rain clouds swirled overhead. To the low spasmodic beat of reggaeton music, their eyes watched him. He averted their gazes and stared at the Bohemia Grande beer in front of him. A few Dominican couples danced. A few more, at other tables, drank, laughed and talked loudly. So loudly, you might think they were fighting. But, no, it's just how they talk. He drank a few mouthfuls and quickly realized a numbing alcohol buzz was starting to dull his senses. But something else was also seeping in; a dull horror at the realization he again had no recollection of what he had done last night, maybe the last few nights. *How many days have I been here? What day is it? What did I do?*

The fear, the memory loss, was almost enough to send him sprinting from the bar in panic. *But, no, be cool, control yourself.* He slowly raised his head and regarded the interested eyes. Six people, half male, half female. Twelve eyes. Eight watching him, the other four dreamily watching each other. An old gringo. A young Dominican woman. In love? In lust? *Money, money, money, I got love in my tummy.* He knew these people.

They were his friends. Costambar wasn't new to him. He had spent time here before. But who the hell were they? What were their names?

"Let me say now, if I offended anyone here last night, I offer a blanket apology," Mac said, while another part of his mind tried to reconstruct recent events. Black pinprick images of debauchery flashed through his mind.

Chuckles around the table. A bellowing laugh.

"Do you know how many times I've heard that around here?" Ryan said. He sipped a Cuba libre from a straw and grinned. "Don't worry, what happens in Costambar stays in Costambar. Everyone gets pie-eyed. Few remember what they did the night before."

"Was I rude?"

"Not too bad," Ryan said. He pointed to the elderly thinning-haired gringo who was now massaging the bare midriff of his slender Dominican date, wife, whatever the hell she was. "You made a pass at Grant's wife, Fanny, but once he reminded you who she was, you backed down."

Grant raised an eyebrow. "Take her off my hands. But it's going to cost you."

"Sorry. Is that all?"

"You told me if I had brains I'd be dangerous," Ryan said. "But I already know that."

A few chuckles. A few knowing glances.

"Sorry again."

Ryan waved it off. "It was a one-night thing. You're usually not that bad when you're drunk; a little sarcastic, a little stupid sometimes, but generally a happy drunk. Not like some I've seen around here. Besides, I told you to fuck off. You seemed to take it in stride—didn't attack me or anything... thank God."

Mac's taught nerves relaxed, but only a little. He looked out at the ocean to try and clear his head. A beautiful bikini-clad Dominican woman sauntered along the beach, smiled at him and resumed her sexy swagger. It didn't take long for the joking conversation to resume, although he was oblivious to its content, lost in his own frantic attempt at recollection. An image had crept into his mind that disturbed him. And he wondered about its validity. Drinking with his friends at the beach bars. Drink, drank, drunk. Then later, back at his apartment. More drinks. A man, perhaps in his mid-fifties, clean cut, good-looking. Caucasian. Canadian? That's right, Canadian. Then, a Dominican woman appears at the apartment, starts having sex with the man, Mac's friend, he's sure; but he can't put a name to the face.

Then, slowly, it comes—Axel McConnely. Then the contents of the drunken conversation:

Mac: "Oh, that's just great. You have a date and I have squat."

Axel: "You can have mine when I'm done."

Mac: "I don't want sloppy seconds."

Axel: "Just don't go down on her. You'll be fine."

Mac: "I don't want sloppy seconds."

Axel: "I'll get you another one."

Mac: "How?"

Axel: "I'll call Frank, my motoconcho."

Mac: "Okay, I want one."

Axel: "You'll get one, don't worry."

A few minutes later, Frank appears, guides Mac out the door, full Cuba libre in hand. Mac climbs on the back of the motorcycle, hangs on with one hand, balances the drink with the other, sipping between bumps in the road. Not a drop spills. Later, a seedy area of Puerto Plata, pitch blackness, but for a lone street light casting a diffused gray light on a shapely and slim female body leaning up against it. Her occupation is obvious. The motoconcho pulls up alongside her and stops.

She smiles.

Frank says, "Do you like her?"

Mac says, "I sure do."

They negotiate a price. The woman climbs on the motoconcho. While Mac continues to drink, without spilling, they drive to an apartment, Mac's apartment.

Inside the room, Mac remembers the sensation. He's wasted, but he remembers moaning and groaning as she gobbles his organ to near-orgasm and then mounts him cowgirl style, pounding him furiously for perhaps twenty minutes. Finally, he climaxes with loud moans and trembling that starts from deep within, slowly dissipating as the orgasm vibrates through his body and out his extremities. *Did I wear a condom? Is it true? Is it my imagination?*

"I thought I saw you in Puerto Plata the other night?" Ryan said.

Mac came back to reality. "In Puerto Plata?"

"Yeah, on a motoconcho. You had a white styrofoam cup in your hand."

Ryan winked. "We'll talk about the details later, when we're not in mixed company."

Mac suddenly felt a pain in his chest. "What day is it?"

"Today's Sunday, January 5th. It's karaoke night."

Mac's mind tilted and tumbled. And he remembered. He had arrived Friday afternoon, January 3rd. What happened after that, other than the debauched drunken night with the hooker, he had no idea. Had he even made contact with Maggie? He felt his body slick with sweat and knew he had to leave these people, and right away. Retreat to his apartment, if he could even remember where he was staying, try to put the missing pieces together, regroup mentally and contact Maggie. And damned quick. He visualized the one night of debauchery. But, some nagging images in the back of his troubled mind told him there were more debauched nights, the details perhaps more sordid.

Mac felt a tap on his shoulder. He swung around, but saw no one. He looked the other way and saw a clean-cut man perhaps in his fifties. Tall. Muscular. Short gray-black hair. Wide smile. Intelligent brown eyes. The name came to him in an instant. "Axel."

Axel put a firm hand on Mac's shoulder. "You look like you've seen a ghost. Come on. Let's go for a walk on the beach. I have to talk to you."

Axel greeted a few people at the table. Mac paid his bill and they left, walking along the beach. The thick layer of clouds was giving way to patches of blue sky, but the wind still whipped strongly, sand-blasting them. Tourists, expats and Dominicans alike, played on the beach, some lazing on bed-style lawn chairs and drinking beer. It was Sunday. Of course the beach would be crowded. It always was. In Canada Sunday might be a day of rest and regrouping for the dreaded Monday morning work-day; but for the Dominicans it was the biggest party day of the week.

Axel asked Mac the details of last night, but Mac offered only perfunctory answers. The realization that the Cuba libre sexcapade was real was haunting him. How many others? He struggled to try and piece together the events of the last two nights, while simultaneously noticing more than the usual amount of smiles from bikini-clad women. He knew why he was getting more looks than normal. It was Maggie's botched spell.

Slowly, his history with Axel permeated a numbed mind, a mind on a dangerous precipice where black insanity beckoned and bellowed from below. They had met three years ago while Mac was vacationing in the DR. Axel was a Canadian military helicopter pilot who had survived being shot down twice during operations in Afghanistan. They had become fast friends, watching one another's backs as situations warranted. They shared the same wacky sense of humor and had many other things in common.

Axel had divorced his trophy wife three years ago after learning her agenda was all about money. The childless marriage had left him tainted and all he wanted to do was enjoy the female fruits of the Dominican Republic. But there had been other conversations. Didn't Axel also mention one day he wanted to find *the one*? Yes. But around here, Axel didn't think that prospect was too likely. He reckoned he might have a five per cent chance of finding a decent woman. The other ninety-five per cent, at least according to Axel, well, they were predators, master manipulators of men's emotions, masters at sucking men emotionally and financially dry. Mac knew at least a dozen men who were sending their "girlfriends" money monthly via Western Union. Many of these "girlfriends" received monthly allowances from other boyfriends as well. Mac knew of one woman, Christina, employed at a beach bar, who it was rumored was receiving money from four different boyfriends totaling $2,500 US a month. When the boyfriends weren't visiting, she was more than happy to turn tricks on the side. Christina didn't view selling her ass as a bad thing. To her, it was the same as selling a pair of shoes only much more profitable. The Dominican bar owner had once commented to Mac, "She makes more money than I do. She doesn't even need this job." Her employer had no problem with Christina turning tricks with customers. On the contrary, he encouraged it and probably got a piece of the action.

"After you left last night, when I was finished with what's-her-name, I called Jillian," Axel said.

Jillian was a mainstream hooker with at least ten years of experience; five years working a brothel, another five years turning tricks at beach bars in Puerto Plata and Costambar. She drank a lot, did a lot of coke, and often displayed a volatile and violent temperament when she was wasted. Axel had a history with her. She was in love with him, or so she said, and vowed to give up her life on the streets if he committed to her whole-heartedly. In reality, Axel probably had a better chance of winning the lottery than getting Jillian off the streets.

Mac turned and stopped. "You did? I hope you're not falling for any of her bullshit."

"I'm trying not to, but it's not easy." Axel gazed at a large-breasted woman, who had just removed her bikini top and covered her melons with a towel, but not before proudly displaying her ample assets. "She ended up sleeping over."

"Did you do her?"

"I can't remember."

Apparently memory lapse, in this case related to alcohol blackout, was more common than Mac would have liked to think. It made him feel marginally better to think many people, Voodoo-spell related or alcohol-induced, suffered from similar problems. "You don't know if you did her?"

"I don't know, bro. We were both naked when I woke up, so probably. Before she left, she told me how much she loved me. You know, she even wears a silver necklace with the letter A. She told me she wants to tattoo my name on her ass."

Mac couldn't help a small chuckle. It emerged like the cackle from an insane mind. Axel raised his eyebrows.

A few beach-heads turned, eyeing Mac curiously.

"At least if she tells you to kiss her ass, you'll know where to start," Mac said, realizing as soon as he said it how lame it sounded.

"She can kiss my fucking ass if she doesn't straighten out."

They sat down at a beach bar, under the shade of an almond tree. A waitress came and Axel ordered two Bohemia Grandes. The beer arrived. Whilst getting sand-blasted, they watched the frolickers playing in the pounding surf. And drank.

"What do you mean, straighten out?" Mac finally asked.

"Before she left, she asked me if I had brought her a smart phone from Canada. I never promised her a smart phone, so I said no. She got pissed off and stormed out of the apartment. But obviously not before taking the 1,500 hundred pesos I offered her."

"You better be careful with that one. Don't believe anything she says. Like most of them around here, her agenda is all money."

"I know, but I have emotions, you know. Sometimes it feels real..." Axel trailed off as an attractive redhead walked gracefully past, casting him an inviting look.

Seeing her, some fleeting recollection flashed through Mac's mind but the fragmented thought disappeared before forming into anything tangible.

"Now that's hot," Axel said, standing up and pointing to her tight little ass and long legs. "Maybe you're right. Maybe I have a better chance at finding quality with a first-world woman."

"You tried that, remember?" Mac quickly bit his tongue. He knew Axel was still smarting from his divorce. The last thing he wanted to do was remind him of it. Besides, the reality was Axel probably did stand a better chance of relationship success, if that's what he wanted, with someone of a similar educational and cultural background.

"Hang on a sec," Axel said, grabbing his beer and marching off toward the sauntering babe. "I'm going to go talk to her."

Before he reached her, Mac could already see her turning around and smiling widely with a perfect set of white teeth. He retched. A wave of nausea swept through his body and he fought the urge to vomit.

He almost tipped over in the plastic chair with surprise when his Dominican phone rang. He didn't remember doing it, but he had obviously activated his travel cell phone after arriving in Puerto Plata. The hairs on his neck stiffened and a cold chill swept over him. It was 104 degrees Fahrenheit in the shade.

What else didn't he remember?

He saw Maggie's name appear on the display and answered it. After the cursory niceties, she said, "I'm calling to remind you of our appointment tonight at nine. Meet me in my office by the gates."

"I remember," Mac lied. He said goodbye and hung up. The cold chill on the back of his neck clung to him like pneumonia.

He checked the phone's contacts. Ten-odd names, most of them female, none forming a mental picture. How many were hookers, how many friends? He saw Axel's number and quickly phoned. Axel, alongside the redhead, had found a spot under a coconut tree (Didn't hundreds of people die every year from coconuts falling from trees?) about a hundred feet away. They talked animatedly. Who the hell was she?

"Listen," Mac said, after Axel answered, "I'm heading home for a nap. I need to regroup. I'll catch up with you later."

"No problem, bro. Let's get into some more trouble later."

"This is a stupid question, but where do I live?"

There was a long pause.

"Wow, I thought I was bad... you're in the Toucan One. Unit eight and, just so you know, I'm in the Toucan Two, number ten."

Mac hung up, paid the bill, grabbed his beer, and walked down the beach. Cackling echoed through his head. The sun emerged from the clouds, blinding him and burning his sensitive pale skin. He staggered, regained his composure and continued.

It should have been just another day in paradise but it was beginning to feel like a day in the bowels of hell. He thought of Axel's name tattooed on Jillian's ass and laughed hysterically. Heads turned, brows furrowed and mocking laughter commenced.

Although he felt helpless to stop it, he knew the evil power inside him was strengthening. And although one part of him was as terrified as a helpless mouse being mauled to death by a cat, another part of him, the part he didn't ever want to admit even existed, was actually starting to like it. At odds with this feeling, Mac began running back to his apartment, Pink Floyd's song *Brain Damage* echoing loudly in his head:

The lunatic is in the hall.
The lunatics are in my hall.
The paper holds their folded faces to the floor
And every day the paper boy brings more.
And if the dam breaks open many years too soon
And if there is no room upon the hill
And if your head explodes with dark forebodings too
I'll see you on the dark side of the moon.
The lunatic is in my head.
The lunatic is in my head
You raise the blade, you make the change
You re-arrange me 'til I'm sane.
You lock the door
And throw away the key
There's someone in my head but it's not me.

Mac wasn't smiling.

He was frowning.

Chapter Thirteen

In that crossroads between life and death, that ineffable realm of existence where many claim to have witnessed a white glowing light of salvation and where others close to being snatched away by the hand of death claim to have witnessed nothing more than a terrifying black abyss, Kalfu, the spirit or Loa of that crossroads, a feared and respected grand master of charms, sorcery and some say black magic, sat cross-legged and frowned.

Six candles in the dungeon-like cave, in the crossroads, barely illumed his black top hat, chiseled features and shiny black slits for eyes. His black spear-like tongue darted out, danced across his blood-red skin and retracted. He drank from a bottle of rum and offered it to the Loa sitting across from him, the Baron Samedi, the spirit of resurrection and the dead. The Baron wore a black tuxedo with a dark blue top hat. His face was a white skull with empty black eye sockets. Chunks of cotton-baton were stuffed into his nose cavity. A lit cigar dangled from his mouth, its blue smoke lazily twirling up, barely visible in the dimly lit cave.

The Baron received the bottle with a skeletal hand and took a long swill on it, grinning wickedly.

Thunder boomed and lightning streaked across the sky. Walls of water poured out of the heavens and over the roof of the cave. The sound and the fury were deafening. The cave shook and trembled with the force. Bits of dust, dirt and tiny pebbles dislodged from the walls and ceiling and crumbled to the ground.

Kalfu ignored it all and stared daggers at the Baron. He had a purpose here and it was time to get down to it. He had plied the Baron with enough liquor while they discussed life, the great beyond, and the often hapless human condition. They might have even solved some of humankind's problems, but this theme had run its course. At least for now. The conversation was becoming circular. The human condition could wait. There was a more pressing matter at hand. Kalfu knew he would have to be diplomatic, even though it wasn't in his nature. But, he would have to make an exception. At least one. Even though he didn't doubt his power over the Baron, he also knew the Loa was capable of disruption, obscenity and debauchery. He would have to tread carefully. Finally Kalfu broke the relative silence. "I did not give you free reign over this lost soul called Mac."

The Baron took another gulp from the half-full rum bottle and a long drag on the cigar. Grinning, he blew a perfect circle into the air that elongated and drifted toward Kalfu. "Well someone sure as fuck did. Otherwise I wouldn't be popping in and out of him like a Jack-in-the-box."

Kalfu swatted the smoke ring with a lightning-swift wave of his hand. It fragmented and drifted away. "You mean to tell me you're not doing this intentionally?"

"I'd be bullshitting you if I said that. And you can tell shit from Shinola."

Kalfu ignored the sarcasm, eager to get to the bottom of this and dispense with the Baron. "So, what is it then? Some of it you're doing intentionally and sometimes you're driven to it by some unknown force?"

"You got it, brother," the Baron said, blowing three more perfect smoke rings. "You know I'm master of many Loa, but someone is undermining me."

"Who?" Kalfu waved away the floating smoke rings. They were starting to annoy him. He had a pretty good idea who was perverting the tenants of Voodoo, but he wanted it confirmed by the Baron.

"Do you know Magdeline Ortega?" the Baron asked, taking another swill of rum and passing the bottle to Kalfu.

Kalfu waved off the bottle. "The woman who claims to be a Voodoo witch. I know of her. I hear she's profiting from Voodoo. This is not what our religion is about."

"I agree with you, Kalfu. But it appears she cast a spell on this Mac person. That spell is causing me to possess him occasionally. Although, I have to admit, the possession is bringing about carnal pleasure the likes of which I haven't experienced in a long fucking time. Do you know how many Dominican women I've fucked in the last two days?"

"I don't care to hear your totals right now," Kalfu snapped.

He was losing patience. He was about to rail on the Baron but bit his slithery tongue and thought. It would do no good to anger this spirit, especially since he controlled the powerful Guede family of Loa and essentially controlled death and resurrection. Besides, it wasn't only the Baron who had been mounting or possessing Mac. Kalfu, although reticent to admit it, had also been influenced by Maggie's spell and had occasionally found himself possessing Mac's body and mind, humping away furiously and deliciously on some attractive Dominican woman. He wondered if it had been Maggie's spell that had possessed him to possess Mac or his own inner need for lasciviousness and debauchery—or his need for revenge. It was troubling indeed. Troubling, because Kalfu never thought it possible for the powers of mortals to become stronger than or interfere with the powers of the Loa. It was the Loa, while possessing human bodies during a Voodoo ceremony, who would mete out good or bad fortune to the families as they saw fit. But mortals gaining some influence over the spirits, being able to put the Loa under spells and make them do their bidding, that was quite another story; one that had the potential to throw the whole pantheon of deities into an uproar and possibly send them on a murderous rampage that could affect hundreds, if not millions of followers.

Recollecting how it all started, Kalfu realized it was partly his fault. During Maggie's initial love spell, he had possessed Mac and quite liked the idea of leaving the island of Hispaniola and fulfilling his carnal desires on Prince Edward Island. Crossing boundaries, crossing borders, to sample the pearly white flesh of a beautiful young Canadian woman. And it had been satisfying. But had he gone too far? Now, it seemed Maggie's spell was drawing in other spirits. At least the Baron had admitted falling victim to it. Was he the only one?

Kalfu couldn't be sure, but he thought so. How would Bondye, the Supreme Being, the Supreme God, react if he learned Kalfu was tampering with witchcraft? Never mind the other Loa, Bondye had the power to terminate spirits and send them deep into the underworld where they would suffer in exile, in incarcerated squalor for all eternity. That can't happen, Kalfu thought.

And that thought led to a plan. He grinned and licked his lips. The answer to his problems was sitting right in front of him, drunker than a skunk, grinning and blowing silly smoke rings. In an instant, he had a scapegoat.

"It seems to me you trailed off," the Baron said, breaking the long silence. "And I would advise you not to get caustic with me."

"I'm sorry," Kalfu said, looking at the near-empty bottle.

Kalfu cupped a hand and another full one magically appeared. It was time for more rum. He and the Baron had that much in common—debauchery and drinking. Kalfu focused on the cap and it spun off and rocketed through the air, bouncing with a tin-like sound off the rock walls.

The night had grown quiet.

He took a long pull on the rum and offered it to the Baron, who polished off what little remained in his bottle and grabbed it eagerly, taking a guzzle, wiping a bony chin and grinning. "Thank you. Don't mind if I do?"

After a moment, the Baron said, "You were saying?"

Kalfu adjusted his tone. It was almost paternal. "I'm not concerned about your totals but what I would like you to do is keep visiting this lost soul called Mac. Fuck him to death if he's not worthy. You decide if he deserves to die or be resurrected. That's your area of expertise anyway. Do your job."

The Baron stood. "Is that why you called me here tonight? Because, if we're done, I have ceremonies to attend, people to save, people to kill. Besides, the peasants are offering more rum and even a sacrificial bull. I could use some bull blood, for fuck sakes. Keeps me young and virile, if you know what I mean."

Kalfu stood and extended a conciliatory hand.

The Baron shook it with a bony hand and grinned.

"It's always good to see you, Baron Samedi," Kalfu said. "I believe we went some way to solving the world's problems tonight."

A little more rum and we just might have."

"True enough. I too have ceremonies to attend and one of them in particular may involve invoking the evil Loa. Someone reluctantly might have to die."

"If that happens, you know how to reach me."

Kalfu released the Baron's hand and grinned. "I sure do. Now, go, do your work."

As the Baron disappeared, Kalfu rubbed his hands together. This just might work out after all, he thought. Someone else would pay for his playful experimentation with a love spell; experimentation that had clearly gotten the better of his own will.

A spirit he detested was going to get banished to the underworld; a life of hell, for a spirit befitting the punishment.

And, as collateral damage, a few people would have to die.

Chapter Fourteen

One part of Mac was dying to know why Maggie had abruptly cancelled the nine o'clock that evening, the other part didn't care. He sat on the balcony of the Toucan One, watching the fireworks blast off from Ocean World—a black sky illuminated with brilliant circular shapes. The stars twinkled as he sipped a rum and Coke and smoked a Marlboro Light. It had rained barrels earlier in the evening, but now the night was calm, still and hot. Sure the fireworks popped, children still shouted and played on the street below, Salsa music blasted from a stereo in the Dominican and Haitian-occupied apartment building next door, the odd dog barked occasionally and the odd motoconcho roared by on the main drag less, than a half a block away; but that was the Dominican Republic. It was relative calm compared to some barrios in Puerto Plata, where noise pollution was deafeningly disruptive.

Returning home earlier in the afternoon, Mac had tried to piece the events of the last two days together with only marginal success. He vaguely remembered what he now called the Cuba libre girl, and at times fleeting glimpses of other carnal rendezvouses would flash through his mind. But the details were scant, save for the odd vision of a desirous nude body, a pair of stunning brown eyes, a perfect smile, a seductive glance, shapely breasts, a nice ass parading around his bed. Heavy breathing, ejaculating, moaning. Problem was, the images would disappear soon after they appeared, leaving him aching for more sex.

Perhaps the empty rum bottles, the many used condoms and wrappers scattered bedside, should have frightened him, but it wasn't so. He was evidently fucking like a rabbit, but could hardly remember the women. It only made him crave more. He hoped he would remember next time.

And that was the physical evidence. There was electronic evidence too. He had at least ten women's phone numbers in his contact list. Scrolling through his phone, he found various text messages from different women; albeit poorly spelled, but discernable enough:

I had a great evening. I love you, Mac. Call me.

I want to see you again. It's not your money I'm after. If you don't have any money, I still want to see you.

How are you? I send you many kisses, my love.

My Mother is sick. I need 2000 pesos.

I'm in the hospital. Call me.

My birthday is next week at El Carey bar. Please come. And bring a nice gift.

Can I borrow two thousand pesos from you? I'll pay you back next week.

My moto can't find the Toucan One. Where is it?

I want to see you tonight. But, first please put 300 pesos on my phone.

I desire to make love to you tonight. We make a great couple. xxx

Call me Mac. I'm out of phone minutes.

I need to talk to you. It's important.

This is my Mother's number. Call me on this phone.

I want to invite you to meet my family. I love you.

Could you buy me a new phone? I lost mine.

You're a great boyfriend. I couldn't ask for anything more.

It seemed, in the short time he had been here, he already had at least one girlfriend by the name of Ilianny.

Mac went inside, refreshed his drink, and returned to the balcony. He scrolled through his phone contacts, found Axel, and dialed. Axel had called earlier, filling him in on the details of a wild sexual encounter with Livia, the Canadian woman he had met on the beach. Axel claimed, in the one week he had been here, Livia performed better sexually than any of his Dominican hookers. But there was a red flag, Mac thought, as Axel answered on the second ring. Livia was saying she loved him already.

"You want to go to La Canita?" Axel said immediately. He didn't bother with social niceties. It wasn't his style.

"What's La Canita?"

"It's a disco in the San Felipe barrio of Puerto Plata. Lots of hotties... many that aren't hookers, if you're looking for something different."

"Is it dangerous?"

"It's not the best barrio. But you're seasoned. You can handle it and besides, what the fuck are we doing here if we can't have a fucking adventure?"

Mac couldn't resist chuckling at his own question. Somewhere in the still-logical recesses of his mind, he felt a tinge of fear and a certainty that the real danger was yet to come. And, as if to confirm the gut instinct, a lyric, from CCR's *Bad Moon Rising*, popped into his head:

Don't go out tonight, they're bound to take your life
There's a bad moon on the rise
Don't go out tonight, they're bound to take your life

There's a bad moon on the rise

What did he have to lose? He was already fucked. *You're fucked now.* But there was some consolation knowing the depression demons had at least temporarily abandoned his soul.

"What the hell," Mac said. "Why not?"

"K, I'll pick you up in fifteen. You'll be ready?"

"Yes."

Mac hung up.

Twenty minutes later, they departed the gates of Costambar, in Axel's rented 1995 white Ford Bronco XLT, both sipping Cuba libres from styrofoam cups. A few people, including four strolling, sexily dressed Dominican women, waved to them and smiled as they left.

Even through his alcoholic haze, Mac could tell Axel was already drunk. Axel probably started drinking on the beach at about nine in the morning, not unusual when he was on vacation. Axel talked about the women.

"How many girls have you fucked since you've been here?"

"I don't know. You?"

"Not sure. But I think it's seven. Some, I was too drunk to remember. Not sure I was able to get it up."

"You still using Viagra?"

"Yeah... I don't really need it, but it enhances the performance. Want a couple?"

Mac extended a hand. "Sure, why not?"

Axel reached into his pocket, extracted two pills, and handed them over.

"Thanks." Mac put them in the zippered pocket of his travel pants.

"I want to warn you about La Canita," Axel said. "First of all, don't deal with more than one waiter. That's when things get fucked up. They already pad the bill for gringos, but if you use more than one waiter it confuses the hell out of them. You could end up paying double. And when we order a bottle of rum, we pay for it right away, that way it's harder for them to upcharge."

"Okay."

"The other thing, don't fall for any of the hustlers outside the bar. Some speak English and they'll tell you they have girls for you, blah, blah, blah. They'll bum smokes, they'll ask you if you want marijuana or coke. Don't accept. Politely tell them to fuck off, tell them you have your own connections, whatever."

"Okay." Mac felt some of his travel instincts coming back. He had heard these stories before, just couldn't remember them, until now.

"You okay?" Axel suddenly asked.

"I'm fine. Drunk."

"Me too, but we'll be okay. You gonna get a girl tonight?"

"I think so."

"Me too."

"Hey, you said things went well with Livia?"

"Yeah."

"She's good in bed?"

"A dynamo"

"Dynamo hums?"

"Oh yeah. Real fine, bro. Real fine."

"There's something about her I don't like."

"What's that?"

"I don't know yet... but it'll come to me. Have you asked anyone here about her history?"

"Not yet... but I'll get the skinny tomorrow."

"I hope so. She leaves a bad taste in my mouth."

"Maybe it's your last hooker's pussy. A little fishy?"

"Never mind. Just be careful."

"I will. Don't worry."

******

A few minutes later, they sat in La Canita, backs against the wall of the open bar, watching people gyrate to the local music on the dance floor. The music was so loud they had to practically yell to be heard. A colorfully illuminated disco ball rotated above them, casting multiple colors onto moving bodies. Between sips of Cuba libres (they had ordered servicio, a small bottle of local white rum, small bottle of Coke and plenty of ice) they talked.

"Do you see anything you like?" Axel said.

Mac pointed to a nearby table of six women. At least two of them occasionally glancing approvingly their way. "I like that one with the long black hair. The one with the white shorts."

"She looks good. I'll take her friend."

Her friend was a petite thing with long golden hair.

"Give me a chance to work up my nerve and I'll ask her to dance," Mac said.

"Don't wait too long... someone else will move in."

A few minutes later, Mac was about approach her table, but he was a little too late. A Dominican man took her hand and led her onto the dance floor. She danced very well, as did he.

"You missed your chance," Axel said.

"She'll sit down. Don't worry. Go ask the other one."

Axel shook his head. "I'll wait for you. I'll be the wing man."

Mac nodded, lit another smoke, and waited for White-Shorts to sit. After twenty minutes, another opportunity presented itself. Mac didn't waste any time approaching the table.

"Would you like to dance?" he asked in Spanish.

She smiled, stood, and they danced. Mac fumbled his way through the Salsa music while White-Shorts gyrated in perfect timing to the beat.

Axel, with White-Shorts' friend, joined Mac on the dance floor.

After two songs, they finished.

Axel sat down at their original table, while Mac joined the six women.

"Hi, I'm Mac. Thanks for the dance."

"I'm Yulissa," White –Shorts said.

"You wanna join us at our table?"

She smiled. "In a minute or two."

Mac returned to his table. As he sat down, Axel grinned, got up, approached the table where his dance partner sat, had a brief conversation, and joined Mac.

They picked up their drinks and toasted.

"I invited Yasmilka over," Axel said. "What about you?"

"Her name's Yulissa. Yeah, I did."

It wasn't long before the two women joined them for drinks.

Mac didn't waste any time. With Yulissa's enthusiastic permission, he logged her name and number into his phone. He spelled it Yulissa Lacanita as a reminder.

"Let's have a toast," Axel said. "To a great time tonight for all of us."

Just then, pandemonium erupted.

A fight between Dominicans broke out at the far corner of the bar, near the bathrooms. One, two, three, four—Mac couldn't be exactly sure, it was so dark and he was so drunk. In the next instance, panicked people were rushing to the entrance en masse.

The table in front of Mac suddenly became airborne and beer bottles and drinks went smashing to the concrete floor. Mac instinctually picked up a chair, held it in front of his face like a shield, and backed against the wall.

As bottles, chairs and tables flew, Axel copied Mac.

Yasmilka fled.

Yulissa was pressed to the wall alongside Mac. He grabbed her by the wrist. People were stampeding past, a fleeing mob mentality.

"Stay here," Mac said, "until this calms down."

"We need to get out," Yulissa shouted, panic-stricken. She tugged Mac's wrist. "Let's go."

Mac pulled her back. "Wait!"

Out of the corner of his eye, he saw a flying object and redirected the chair. A full beer bottle hit it and shattered, broken glass flying everywhere. Then another. And another. And another. Beside him, Axel also dodged and blocked flying beer bottles.

A few seconds later it was all over. Most of the people had fled and objects stopped flying. Only a few stragglers remained.

Amid shouts and screams, Mac saw one man staggering out of the bar, hand covering a bloodied head.

"I lost my cell phone," one woman shouted. "Someone stole it."

"My purse is gone," another said. "Someone robbed me."

Mac still held Yulissa's hand. She was frozen with fear.

Mac turned to Axel. "Now, let's get the hell out of here." Mac locked eyes with Yulissa. "Let's go," he said, leading her out.

They walked carefully through a sea of spilled drinks, broken glass, shattered chairs and tables. Once outside they were pushed into a thick crowd and barely able to move. Motorcycles and cars roared in from every direction, picking up fleeing patrons.

Yulissa bent down and started gathering coins that had spilled out onto the street.

Mac released her hand. "What're you doing? Let's get out of here."

She glanced up at him sorrowfully but continued the spare-change hunt.

Axel yanked Mac's arm. "Let's go," he shouted. "Before another fight breaks out."

Mac followed Axel's lead and headed to the Bronco. Weaving between traffic, they crossed the street.

A dark and disheveled man followed them to the car, holding out a hand and demanding money for watching the vehicle.

Beside the Bronco, three women stood, cackling and pointing at the crowd in front of the bar. Mac followed their fingers and noticed another fist-fight had broken out between two Dominicans. One man swung at another with a broken beer bottle. A circle formed around the combatants.

Axel was now inside the vehicle, while Mac stood outside and watched. The disheveled man grabbed him roughly by the arm.

"Give me some money for watching the car."

"Tell him to fuck off," Axel said. "Get in. NOW!"

Mac saw much suffering in the beggar's eyes. He reached into his pocket, extracted a hundred peso note, and handed it to him. Releasing Mac's arm, the man beamed with joy.

"Thank you. Thank you so much."

Mac climbed into the vehicle and slammed the door.

"Look," Axel said, pointing down the street a ways. "That's Yasmilka."

She stood on a nearby curb, talking to an elderly man.

Axel started the Bronco, backed out, and pulled forward, stopping in front of them and rolling down his window. "You okay?"

She nodded. "It's my father. He wants me to come home now."

The mobs circling the combatants split momentarily and the two emerged. One, still armed with the broken beer bottle, chased the other down the street. They disappeared around a corner.

"No problem," Axel said. "I'll call you okay?"

Yasmilka nodded.

Axel waved, rolled up the window, and slowly rolled forward.

Yulissa emerged from the crowd and approached the passenger side window, where Mac watched the crowd slowly begin to disperse. Mac rolled down the window.

"Aren't you going to take me home tonight?" she asked.

For the first time, Mac became aware that his heart was beating furiously in his chest and his hands were trembling. The adrenaline rush was going full-throttle. "I don't think so. Not tonight. This whole incident freaked me out. I'll call you though, okay?"

She nodded and forced a smile. She was visibly trembling.

They suddenly heard police sirens.

"It's time," Axel said, pulling away quickly.

They were silent for a few minutes as he weaved his way down a few side streets and out of the mayhem.

Mac was at a loss for words. Some of the fear he felt earlier was returning. There were things he hadn't told Axel, like he was under some weird Voodoo spell that was definitely veering sideways. There was more. The nightmares, the impending sensation of things getting worse. Maybe it was time to enlighten his friend. *In his alcohol-induced condition? Are you kidding? Give your head a shake. He won't remember fuck all, probably won't remember most of the evening. Another time, when and if you can catch him sober.*

So instead, Mac asked, "Where to now?"

"To the Malecon," Axel said without hesitation. "Let's go to Raffi's and see what kind of shit we can stir up."

"You're driving."

******

Bellied up at the bar a few minutes later, an attractive waitress flirted with Mac, smiling, winking, twice even gently touching his leg. He returned the favor by stroking Manuela's bare leg. She didn't seem to mind.

Axel gave Manuela an approving glance as she left to serve other customers. "You could do a lot worse."

Two Haitian women, both dressed in dark red mini-skirts, saddled up to the bar next to them. Initially, Mac was resistant to their company but another large Bohemia changed all that. Before long, they bought the women drinks and engaged them in conversation. Rossy and Violeta had one thing on their minds; they wanted company for the night.

Rossy sat close to Axel and slowly walked her fingers toward his crotch.

Violeta talked with Mac animatedly and smiled often. Occasionally, she touched his hand, gauging his level of resistance. As he flicked a cigarette ash, she slid her long and sharp fingernails gently across the top of his hand.

"You want to go home with me?" she asked.

Mac knew better than to engage in negotiation unless he was willing to participate. He paused at the question, letting Carnality and Reason wage a brief battle in his mind. It was only thirty-three seconds into the first round when Carnality landed a knock-out blow to the underdog, Reason.

"How much do you want for the night?"

"Two thousand pesos."

"I don't pay that. Try a thousand."

"Fifteen hundred."

"It's a thousand, or we leave without you."

Violeta quickly nodded.

"How much is she willing to take?" Axel asked.

"A thousand."

"So is this one. Let's do it."

"You sure?" Mac asked.

Reason crawled along the canvass, reaching a wobbly hand to the ropes for support.

"Of course. Let's go have a pool party."

******

They left the beach bar shortly after negotiations were completed and arrived at the Toucan One. Mac brought down a stereo, a large bottle of rum, a two-liter bottle of Coke, a bucket of ice (even in the haze of arriving he remembered to get the staples) and away they went; dancing, drinking, having sex in various positions in the pool, on the outdoor furniture and patio. A few hours later, they made what appeared to be a grand decision— a foursome in Mac's apartment.

The recent past erased from his memory, Mac laid on his back while Violeta gyrated on top to the pulse of his throbbing member. He opened his eyes for what he thought was the first time since they had arrived there, and watched her movements. She grinned with pleasure.

Mac glanced beside him, where Rossy's head was a few inches from his chest. She panted and moaned with pleasure while Axel pumped her doggie-style.

Axel slapped Rossy's ass hard. "Take it, you bitch. That's it... take it." Then he looked at Mac. "You're fucking her. I can't believe my brother is fucking her." He held out his hand in the high-five gesture. "Gimme five, bro... we got it going on."

Mac slapped his hand and continued. Violeta's head lolled to one side for a second. Mac thought she was going to pass out from too much drink. He wondered how much he had consumed as he continued pumping her, at the same time trying to focus on getting off for fear his member would lose interest if he got too distracted, especially combined with all the booze. But he was remembering, he kept telling himself. That was a good thing.

"Remember what we agreed," Rossy said, as she pumped away. "Two thousand each. That's what you said."

"We agreed on a thousand each," he said, feeling his member soften like a water-logged Twinkie. He gently pushed her off, turning to Axel. "Did you hear what she said? She wants two thousand each. That's not what we agreed to."

Mac dressed quickly and left the bedroom.

Axel followed.

"I'm not giving these girls two thousand each," Mac said.

"I don't blame you. I don't have two thousand on me. I spent everything. I only have a thousand."

Mac fished though his pockets and dug out twelve hundred pesos. He had no idea if there was more money in the bedroom closet safe or not, but wouldn't dare check now, with the two women in there.

Violeta entered the living room, lit a smoke, poured a Cuba libre—about ten ounces of rum and a half ounce of Coke—drained three quarters of it and reclined on the couch, completely nude, smoking a cigarette.

"You assholes pay us two thousand each like you agreed," she demanded.

Rossy, fully clothed, entered the room and sat on an adjoining love seat, silently watching her friend.

"We negotiated a thousand each," Mac said. "And keep your voice down. It's almost six in the morning."

"I want two thousand pesos and I'm not leaving until I get it," Violeta shouted, louder than her first outburst. She polished off her drink, rose to her feet, poured another of equal strength, sat down again, took a large swill, set the styrofoam cup on the coffee table, smoked her cigarette and sulked.

Mac turned to Axel. "Give me your thousand and let's get rid of them."

Axel handed the thousand over. "I think I'm getting out of here."

"No, stay. Please. Don't leave me here with these two. I have no idea what'll happen."

Axel nodded.

Mac added his twelve hundred to Axel's thousand and approached Rossy, who had remained calm during Violeta's outburst. He waved the money. "Tell her to take a thousand... here's a few hundred for a motoconcho... please get her out of here."

Rossy tried to convince Violeta, who only shook her head and grew angrier.

"I'm not leaving here until they pay us two thousand pesos," Violeta said. "I'm going to call the cops."

She polished off her drink, stood, lost her balance, crashed onto the coffee table and rolled onto the floor. A trailing alcoholic beverage followed her, spilling its sticky contents on her face. Cigarette butts and ashes, sent airborne by the impact, also landed on her face, making her look like some absurd anti-smoking advertisement.

Axel began guffawing.

Mac had to bite his lip to contain a fit of laughter.

Even Rossy was smiling, as she helped her friend up and led her, staggering and mumbling, into the bathroom. She closed the door behind her and Mac heard the shower running.

"Please, stay with me until we get this solved," Mac pleaded. "I have no idea what these women are capable of."

"I will. Don't worry."

Suddenly, a shout from a neighbor below: "Would you keep the goddamned noise down?"

Mac quickly closed the balcony door and brought his voice to a whisper. "The neighbors are getting pissed."

"Fuck them... it's the DR. What do they expect?"

"Axel... I have to live with these people, for who knows how long."

No answer.

They were quiet for a few minutes. Then Violeta entered the living room, still nude, but dripping wet from the shower. Shouting Spanish obscenities, she walked straight into a wall and collapsed on the floor.

Mac approached her. Bending down, he noticed a goose-egg growing from her forehead and a small cut trickling blood. Rossy entered and shrugged her shoulders, as much as to say, I want to take the money and go, but what can I do?

Mac felt Violeta's neck for a pulse. There was one. He sighed. "Help me put her to bed. We can't put her out on the street like this. If she falls and kills herself, we're in deep shit."

They put her to bed and piled in beside her. Four people in a double bed. One big happy family.

Axel passed out almost immediately and began snoring loudly.

Soon, Violeta joined the snoring chorus.

Rossy, next to Mac, was silent, eyes wide open. Just like Mac's.

Sleep would not come; too much worry, too much fear. And there was too much fucking nasally snoring going on around here. Silently he stared at the ceiling, watching the slow undulating movements of the ceiling fan above, tinted misty gray by strands of stray moonlight. He heard squawking of first one, then two, then three roosters proclaiming the dawn of a new day. *The dawn of a new day,* he thought. *The dawn of a new dead.*

******

Not far away, in a rough and ready barrio of Puerto Plata called San Marcos, a Swiss woman, Estella Verbeek, a twenty-year expat, snored peacefully, curled up on the living room couch of her second-floor apartment. On the television in front of her a Spanish novella played. A man armed with a gun approached a woman in a dark alley. The woman screamed. He shot her in the head and she dropped to the ground.

Outside the bathroom window of the apartment, a masked man with a knife silently sliced the bathroom window screen. He quietly removed the glass window slats, bent the frame easily and climbed in. He walked into the living room, admired sleeping Estella for a few moments and went into the bedroom.

He returned with a pillow and placed it over Estella's head. He extracted a handgun, aimed it at the pillow, and blasted it twice. Muffled gunshots echoed through the room. Outside, a dog barked.

He lifted the blood-soaked pillow and threw it on the floor. He stood back to admire his work as feathers drifted to the floor. Two drops of blood dripped from Estella's nose, stopping at her lips. Her mouth popped open. Rivulets of blood drained out, down her neck and onto her bosom. He removed the mask and stuffed it into his pocket. The whites of his eyes glowed red in contrast to his dark face.

He robbed the apartment, unlocked the front door and left.

The man would never be caught. The case would never be solved.

******

Not far away in the town of Sosua, a sixty-something Italian expat named Guido Palermo left his small house where he had lived for twenty-four years, got in his car and pulled out of his driveway, on his way to the store to purchase milk for his morning coffee.

Not a block later, he stopped after spotting an injured puppy squirming in the middle of the road. He left his car and rushed to the canine's aid. As he picked up the bleeding puppy, two Dominican men ran out of some nearby bushes and bludgeoned him repeatedly in the head with lead pipes.

The puppy dropped from his hands, hit the ground, and limped away squealing and whimpering.

Guido fought bravely, but was no match for the thugs. They beat him to a pulp, threw him in the back of his car and, for good measure, tied an electrical extension cord around his neck.

Then they robbed him and disappeared.

The men would never be caught. The case would never be solved.

******

A good distance away, in a small village just outside of Port-au-Prince, Haiti, a villager had been caught raping a nine-year-old girl.

In a Voodoo ceremony filled with wild dance, snake-vertebrae rattles, the frenetic beat of animal-skin drums, and the chants of Voodoo followers, a priest injected the man with a powerful anesthetic derived from the Puffer fish while others held his struggling extremities. The man shook violently for a few seconds and then became completely still. His breathing and heartbeat stopped and he appeared to be dead.

The participants lifted the man, wrapped him in a white blanket, and carried him to a shallow grave, where he was placed inside and buried.

Three days later, he would be exhumed, given a powerful antidote, and be resurrected. But his brain would be severely damaged. He would have lost much of his reasoning power, intelligence, willpower and identity. For all intents and purposes, he would be a zombie.

In this zombified state, he would serve the family of the raped girl for the rest of his life, do their bidding; essentially be at their beck and call for any labor or task they saw fit to assign him. Or, he would be sold into a life of forced labor.

Some might call it a cruel and unusual punishment. Others might call it justice.

******

Not an hour from the gates of Costambar, in a small rural village in the mountains of the Dominican Republic, in a Voodoo ceremony that had endured through the night, the chanting stopped. The houngan's rattle stopped rattling. The cadence of the drumbeat grew faster, louder.

A lean man in a loin cloth, who had been gyrating around a blazing fire, froze on spot. Kalfu swooped down from the spirit world and possessed him, allowing the evil Loa into the ceremony. The man, his eyes turning black, started weeping and began a slow, methodical, zombie-like walk around the fire's perimeter. His muscles swelled. He scooped a dagger off the ground and began waving it threateningly at the circle of congregants.

They didn't flinch, only stared, in fascination and awe at the power of the great spirit.

The man stopped waving the dagger and continued his zombie-like perimeter-fire-walk.

He had personal problems and was appealing to Kalfu to solve them. The grandmaster of sorcerers and charms was also viewed by many as the master of the human condition. The man was married to a loyal woman for twenty years. She had never strayed, never committed infidelity. But, for reasons of his own, he had become fiercely jealous and possessive of her.

Whenever he saw her in the presence of another man, although most times she would only be talking, he would fly into a fit of rage. The fits grew worse until one day he raised a hand in anger and slapped his wife hard across the face; so hard it left a pink hand imprint. When he had calmed down, she vowed to leave him if he didn't change his ways.

The drumbeat grew faster, louder still.

The man stopped suddenly, raising the dagger high into the air. To widening eyes, he pushed the blade slightly into his chest. His expression remained trance-like. Blood squirted from the wound and snaked down his chest, tiny red rivers.

Inside the man, Kalfu sighed. In a fit of anger, he had decided the man was not worthy of salvation or rehabilitation. He wanted to kill him. But, Kalfu suddenly realized. He couldn't do that. Not without the acceptance of the Baron Samedi, the spirit of the dead. And the Baron, he knew, was currently not available. He was fucking like a rabbit inside the body of one MacKenzie Adamson.

Then an idea occurred to Kalfu. This would be the perfect opportunity to check on the Baron without it seeming too obvious. He could report the jealous man's condition and seek the Baron's advice. That would be following the proper spirit protocol. Maybe, the jealous clown he now possessed was a candidate for the punishment of zombification.

Kalfu willed his hands to stop the slow inward progress of the blade. It withdrew from the wound, flew into the air, and landed on the ground, clanging and glittering red in the fiery sunrise.

Kalfu exited the lost soul and ascended high into the sky. There would be another ceremony, another time to deal with this fool.

******

Some time later, Violeta stopped snoring, stirred, opened her eyes and glanced at the bedside clock: 7:36 am.

Mac opened one eye and followed her gaze.

Axel rolled over, fell off the bed, and landed with a loud thud on the ceramic tile floor. He grunted loudly.

Rossy stirred, got up and went to his aid. She helped him back into bed.

From above, the Baron Samedi watched, frowning slightly. He was growing tired of this charade. Sure, he had enjoyed the sex with Violeta, but he couldn't help the feeling that something was wrong with this picture.

Earlier, after his carnal desires were suitably satisfied, he had waited patiently for Kalfu to possess Mac and have his way with these women. But where was Kalfu now? Why, after three consecutive nights possessing Mac was he conspicuously absent?

Something didn't fit. The Baron could feel it in his seasoned bones. So when a small tapping sound was heard at the apartment door and a small voice called, "Violeta, Violeta... are you there?" the Baron took his cue, floated through the ceiling, and disappeared.

******

"Did you hear that?" Mac said to anyone who was listening.

Axel opened an alert military-trained eye. "Someone's at the door."

"I don't think it's here, "Mac said. "It's another apartment."

The knocking again. The voice, again: "Violeta... are you there?"

"It's here," Axel said, getting up and dressing. "Maybe you should answer it."

Mac got out of bed, fumbled around for a t-shirt, found one, put it on, and went to the door.

Axel stood behind him. Mac heard commotion in the bedroom and bathroom. He hoped and prayed the girls were getting ready to leave.

"Who is it?" Mac said.

"It's Dasha. I'm looking for my sister, Violeta."

Mac opened the door and saw a Haitian woman dressed in a white mini-skirt. She entered and, smiling, planted a wet kiss on his lips.

"You're attractive," she said, pulling out a business card and placing it on the coffee table. "I'd like to sleep with you some time. Call me."

Mac nodded.

"Tell me, did Violeta get you off?"

"Yes," Mac said. "Take her home, please?"

"Sure, my love. Where is she?"

Mac pointed to the bedroom.

Dasha went in and closed the door; faint conversation, voices growing louder—yelling and screaming. He hoped he hadn't left any valuables in his room. Around here, valuables grew legs quickly and walked, no ran away.

The arguing from behind the bedroom door grew quiet.

The three women emerged.

Violeta looked no less sober than she had earlier. She staggered to the kitchen counter, filled a styrofoam cup with ninety-eight per cent rum, two per cent Coke, swallowed half of it, and scowled at Mac. "Do you have two thousand pesos for each of us?"

"This is all the money I have," Mac said, approaching and extending a handful of bills. "Please, take it and leave."

Violeta snatched the money from his hand and counted it. "This isn't enough." She pulled out a cell phone. "I'm calling the cops."

"No, you're not," Dasha said, grabbing her sister's arm. "Put that away, give half the money to Rossy and let's go."

Violeta's eyes narrowed. She bunched her fists into balls, glaring at Axel and Mac.

Priceless seconds ticked by. Mac thought for sure this would end badly.

And, just when it appeared Violeta would explode into a violent fit of rage, Dasha said something that instantly calmed her: "Let's go sister. Your baby son Samuel is waiting for you at home and Mother's tired of looking after him."

A look of grudging resignation swept over Violeta's black eyes. She opened her hands, peeled off eleven hundred pesos and handed them to Rossy, who quickly snatched them from her hand. Then Violeta seized the bottle of rum from the counter, took a large swill and staggered to the door, dribbling a trail behind.

Follow the trail, Mac thought stupidly. *It always steers you right.*

When the women left, Mac closed the door and sighed.

"Wait a bit before you leave," Mac told Axel. "You don't want to be accosted on the street by that nutcase."

Chapter Fifteen

Hands cupped to her cheeks, elbows planted on her desk, Maggie sat pensively on a sunny afternoon watching but not seeing the street life outside the small window of her office. She was recollecting the past, trying to come to grips with the present and revisiting her goals and ambitions. They involved Kalfu to a great extent.

She wasn't a big fan of Kalfu. A little stronger than that, actually. She hated the spirit, although she was careful not to cement that hatred into her mind, for fear the powerful spirit would detect it and wreak havoc on her little Costambar parade.

If he already hadn't.

Something was going terribly wrong with her spells and she was sure Kalfu was possessing her clients at random, having his way with multiple women, and leaving the spell victims shattered, shaken and broken, with little or no recollection of the lurid events. But the damage was more than that. Oftentimes, the only urges they were left with were sexual—a need to conquer more women, engage in more sex, satisfy that base and often shallow urge for euphoric bliss.

Maggie had other reasons for disliking the mighty spirit.

The life-altering memory was as clear now as it was then.

She was a little girl of eight years old, living in a tin-roofed shanty town shack in a small impoverished Haitian village. An only child, she lived with her mother Awilda and her Voodoo priest father Carlos. The family depended on donations from villagers to survive. And these donations: food, furniture, offerings of rum and cigarettes and sacrificial animals and blood to appease the Voodoo spirits, were plentiful. The community respected Carlos for his wisdom and ability to call up and communicate with the spirits at random. He had healed many sick, reversed the fortunes of otherwise troubled families, and brought relative peace and happiness to a struggling congregation.

But something had gone terribly wrong during one of Carlos's Voodoo ceremonies. It was summer and stifling hot in the village. Rachel, a twenty-two-year old local woman, had visited Carlos early that morning. She desperately needed his help. She was having sex with multiple men and could barely remember them. She wanted to be cured of her sex addiction, wanted to live a life of fidelity with one special boyfriend, have two-point-five kids and live as happily ever after as her squalid conditions would permit.

Later that evening, Rachel returned. A Voodoo ceremony commenced and Carlos proceeded to invoke Erzulie Freda, the spirit of love, in the hope of curing her. Villagers danced around a blazing fire, Carlos shook the symbolic rattle, the drums beat, the congregation chanted. A goat was sacrificed at a small alter, its blood, along with splashes of rum, spread over it. The animal was decapitated and the worshippers passed its head around, taking turns sucking blood from the protruding veins.

A congregant was suddenly possessed by a spirit. He began dancing around the fire spasmodically, sipping rum from a bottle and spraying mouthfuls into the blaze. Then he stopped, lit two cigarettes, and smoked them rapidly. When he finished, he spread his arms to the heavens and stared, frigid and zombie-like.

Standing behind him, Rachel's eyes brightened. "I'm cured."

The wind intensified and the full moon emerged from behind a dark cloud. Suddenly, Carlos, who had been sitting pensively, was elevated into the air and thrust violently into the fire.

People screamed. Many shouted, "No, no.... nooooooooo, not Carlos." And many, panic stricken, fled.

A human fireball, Carlos staggered out of the blaze. Before he crumpled to the ground and burned to death, he shouted, "Kalfu... why do you do this? Kalfu? Noooooooooooooooooo... oooo... oooo."

Rachel, taking pity on Carlos, dove on his burning body and clung to it. Horrified onlookers, much too fearful to douse the flames, watched the duo meet a fiery death.

Maggie was among the spectators. She buried her face into her hands and sobbed, traumatized. Her father and the woman he cured were dead. Her mother, Awilda, a month later, developed some undiagnosed illness that saw her lose fifty pounds in a week and shrivel away to practically nothing before dying a mere skeleton of her former self.

After that, Maggie, leaning on the black magic side of Voodoo, vowed to devote her life's work to helping people fall in love. And to a very large extent, she had succeeded. But, in the back of her troubled mind, another agenda, a plan she was reluctant to give voice to, was secretly and almost subconsciously forming; she wanted revenge on Kalfu, who she blamed for killing her father. And to execute that revenge, she knew she had to transcend the mortal world and become a Loa, a powerful Voodoo spirit.

It was there, on that elevated plane of existence, that she knew she would have a chance at avenging her father's death. And now, more than ever, the plan had taken on an element of immediacy. Now, because it seemed Kalfu was cognizant of her life's purpose and he was meddling with it.

He was fucking with her.

It was no longer only about revenge. No, not just revenge.

It was a question of self-defense.

It was time to show that meddling spirit monster what would happen to him if he continued to thwart Maggie's success. And to do that, she would start with the spell victims. Make them incapable of succumbing to Kalfu's will. Maybe then, he would begin to understand his limitations. Put him in his place, weaken his power, pass into the spirit realm and execute his demise. *That's the idea, but how to do it is quite another thing,* Maggie thought, as a bell chimed and an eerie squeaking sound announced the arrival of her next client.

Seeing Livia's bright smile did little to alleviate Maggie's somber mood. Including Mac in the love spell with Michael and Pamela had been a mistake. Their relationship, far from improving, was worse than ever. Pamela had attacked Michael on the beach yesterday and almost beat him senseless with a stick.

Kalfu and probably another spirit were having their way with Mac. Fucking with him—fucking like a rabbit through his body.

Livia sat down at Maggie's desk.

Maybe the answer was right here in front of her. Maggie grinned. "Livia, my friend, good to see you. How are you?"

******

Livia locked eyes with Maggie. The two were casual acquaintances at best. Normally, Livia didn't put much stock in Voodoo witchcraft, but lately she had been starting to pay attention to Maggie's love spells. It was hard not to. Word had gotten out about some of her successes. Hell, Livia had witnessed a few good results. But, lately she had also seen some of her failures, particularly the botched spell involving Michael and Pamela and Pamela's violent attack yesterday, striking Michael senseless (*as if the wing nut had any sense anyway*, Livia thought) with a stick.

As she studied Maggie's black, intense eyes, Livia thought she could read an agenda there; she was adept at reading people's true intentions. She hadn't gotten this far, hadn't won so many victories extracting men's emotions and then their hard-earned money, by being a fool. Brad, for example, was fitting into her plans nicely and being played like a string puppet. Unfortunately, he had to leave because of a death in the family; but he would be back and he would be as emotionally frail as a small boy who has just seen his puppy dog get run over by a car. Maybe it was good, a blessing in disguise perhaps. Now, while she waited for Brad's return, she could concentrate on Mac and Axel.

Swallowing a lump in her throat, a gooey remnant of Axel's ejaculate, after this afternoon's fuck-fest, Livia coughed slightly, cleared her throat, and replied. "I'm doing well. What's with you anyway? You look like you've seen a ghost."

"No. I'm just trying to fix some of my... I'm sure you've heard... not so positive results lately with the love spells."

"I don't think Michael's too happy right now. The adjectives he used to describe your practice weren't exactly complimentary—downright profane actually."

"Well, I'm going to fix that. What can I do for you anyway?"

Livia paused while she considered this. She wanted two things. She was worried that Mac might eventually remember her and put the kybosh on her progress with Axel, so his memory of their relationship needed to be erased. Mac's disrespect during their relationship certainly warranted retribution too. A few days ago, she had considered approaching Maggie to put a nasty curse on Mac. But, watching and hearing about his lewd behavior lately, she was convinced it had already happened, without any input on her part. But, before she went any further, she had to be sure.

Secondly, she wanted Maggie to put a spell on Axel. Sure, he had started making love to her regularly, but he was also galavanting around with practically every hooker he could get his dirty little hands on. For Livia to conquer Axel and his money, he had to fall in love with her. And that wasn't happening, at least not fast enough for Livia's liking.

How to approach this?

After a long silence, she spoke: "Maybe we can help each other. If you level with me regarding your clients, actually one in particular, I'll figure out a way to help you with your agenda."

"You don't even know my agenda."

"That suggests you have one. Do you?"

"That's really none of your business."

"Hear me out. Maybe I can make it my business."

"Go ahead. Say your piece and make it quick. I have to get ready for my three-thirty."

Livia initially thought a surreptitious approach would be best. But, she changed her mind and decided to just come right out and say it. "I don't like Mac. He and I had a history. He disrespected me and dumped me in a horrible way. I want my revenge. I was going to come to you earlier, but I didn't for a few reasons. One, I knew your spells involved love, attraction, reconciliation, all kinds of positive shit like that. But, lately I've seen a most unsavory change in some of your spell victims and I've started to wonder if you haven't changed teams..."

Maggie's eyes narrowed and she opened her mouth to speak.

"... Not only that, Maggie. Hear me out. I've also noticed a change in you. The way you act now. The way you talk. You've got some dark plan in your head and maybe now you'll be a little more receptive to what I have to say."

"You're taking a long time to say nothing."

"All right, I'll just say it then. Did you put a spell on Mac?"

"Why would I tell you that?"

"Because if you did, and it's not working, I can help you get rid of the evidence."

"Why would I want to get rid of evidence? I only try to help people."

"Oh, come now. Don't patronize me. If people find out you put a spell on Mac, and that's what's been messing with him, you're in deep kaka. How long do you think it will take before the entire town finds out? Word is already spreading about some of your... excuse the pun... fuck ups."

A long pause.

Finally, Maggie said, "What exactly are you proposing?"

"We make a deal. You put a love spell on Axel—and don't fuck this one up—and I'll get rid of Mac."

"How are you planning on doing that?"

"What you don't know won't incriminate you."

"Are you going to kill him?"

"You heard me."

Another long pause.

Finally Maggie said, "What do you want?"

Livia breathed a deep sigh. This was far from over, but at least now she had a fighting chance, an edge that she didn't have before, at capturing Axel's wealth and stomping his fickle and infidel heart into blood-red pulp.

And, she could finally extract her revenge on that low-life, scum-sucking, bottom-feeding fool, MacKenzie Adamson.

"Close the door and take a seat," Maggie said. "I'll tell you everything and we'll make a deal."

Chapter Sixteen

"Here's the deal," Mac said, swilling a beer. "I judge my self-worth by my intellectual pursuits."

He was at a beachfront bar with seven other expats, most of whom he knew by name, some of whom he considered his friends. One Swiss guy, who called himself Swenson, Mac had never seen or talked to before.

The small wooden-hut beach bar was busy. Of the eight tables on the beach, seven were occupied; some with elderly gentlemen accompanied by much younger beautiful Dominican and Haitian women, others by tourists with colorful wrist bands, markers of the many five-star resorts dotting the Atlantic coast. There was much talk and laughter.

"That's a fucking joke," Michael said, rubbing a cut on his cheek, a battle scar from Pamela's earlier frenzied attack. "What intellectual pursuits? All you've been doing here is drinking beer and fucking. Is being a drunk an intellectual pursuit? Is being a womanizer?"

"You have a point," Mac said, flashes of sordid nights racing through his mind. "I'm a drunk. I'm a womanizer. I'm a fool half the time. But, I'm also an artist. I do editing. I do SEO writing. Both art. At the tail end of all those titles is writer."

"You're only as good as your last words," Tobias Johnson, an American from New York, said. "And what have you written today?"

"Fuck all."

"So that makes you a womanizer, a fool and a drunk," Michael said. "You're only a writer if you write. You haven't written fuck all today."

"Okay," Mac said, raising his glass. "Here's to being a fool, a drunk and a womanizer. I bet there's a lot like me around here."

They toasted and drank. There were a few chuckles and nods.

Mac's eyes traveled to the ocean. The waves gently lapped the shore. The sky was clear and deep blue. A gentle breeze blew in. They sat under the shade of an Almond tree. After Rossy and Violeta had left, Axel had waited a few minutes and disappeared. They both grabbed a few hours of sleep, met at the nearby Anchor for the plate of the day—rice, beans, chicken and salad for 140 pesos—then went to the beach for a day of drinking and solving the world's problems, at least the problems of Costambar and the local culture. Mac had earlier relayed the story of the crazy hookers they had picked up on the Malecon, and how difficult it had been to get rid of them. He watched two bikini-clad shapely women saunter by and it reminded him again of the sordid night that finished early this morning. He frowned.

"Are you okay?" Axel asked.

Mac nodded and swilled beer, hoping the alcohol would clear his head and cure his hangover. *Wishful thinking, buddy. You're in a world of shit.*

"By the way," Leonard Millar, a sixtyish clean-cut Canadian who had lived in Costambar full-time for over eight years, asked, "Did those fuckin cunts do any damage?" A retired oil and gas engineer, he was a take-no-bullshit kind of guy, who told it like it was, like it or not. The word discretion was not part of his colorful vocabulary; although with his friends he was loyal to a fault.

The group fell silent. Sixteen eyes focused on Mac. "One girl burned a large hole in the couch with her cigarette. It's a brand new velvet couch. I'm gonna have to sort it out with the landlord."

"Another thing," Leonard said, "if those bitches threaten to call the cops, tell them *you'll* call the cops. You should put the contact names and numbers of the police in your phone. There's gate security, for example, you can call them. People around here with their taxes pay their salaries to keep trouble out of this community. You watch how fast they put down their phones when you threaten to call the cops. But, ideally you have to do it first. They give you trouble, pick up your phone and say 'I'm calling the cops if you don't fuck off.' And if they don't leave, call the fuckin cops. The natives around here, they all wanna fuck with you. Every time I turn around someone wants to fuck with me. Yesterday, people were trying to fuck with me. Today they're trying to fuck with me. Same shit, different pile."

"I'm sure you've seen a lot," Mac said.

"Oh yeah. I knew an Italian guy, built a house on some land just outside Sosua. Anyway, he finishes it, well nearly anyway. He leaves, has to go home for something, I don't remember what the fuck it was. He comes back a few months later and his entire house is gone. Brick by brick the fuckers stole his whole house."

"Anyone ever tell you, you swear a lot," Toby said with a wry smile.

"Yeah, well fuck you and the ship you came in on," Leonard said, refilling his beer glass.

"It was a horse and I rode in from Santo Domingo."

"I wouldn't doubt it," Leonard said. "You never have any fuckin money."

"That reminds me of a story," Toby said. "I used to have more money. When I first arrived here..."

"What, after they let you out of Rikers Island..."

"They did, but that's another story."

"How many misfits down here have a criminal past and are hiding from the law," Leonard said. "I'll tell you one thing... I got nothing to hide. I'm clean as a fuckin whistle."

"Let me finish my story."

"I'm not stopping you."

"Anyway, seven years ago, I decide to move to Santo Domingo," Toby continued. "I met some Dominican in New York. Tells me he's got some real estate project in the city I should invest in. I do all my due diligence, at least I think I do, go down there and invest a hundred thousand dollars, my entire life savings."

"That's because you're a fucking clown," Leonard said.

Toby scoffed and continued. "This slime ball takes off with my money. Turns out it wasn't even in his name. He was selling someone else's project. Anyway, it all goes tits up. The fucker disappears with my money. So, I'm fuming, ready to kill this bastard. By this time, I've got a wife, a little kid in tow, and not a pot to piss in. So I learn where he lives. One day, mid-afternoon, he leaves his house and comes down the street. I come up behind him with a baseball bat and clobber him over the back of the head as hard as I can."

Toby stood up and gave a pantomime performance of the swing. Some tourists seated nearby turned their heads.

"I mean I nailed this loser. I hit a fuckin home run. Right out of the damn park. He drops like a sack of hammers and I clobber him twice more with the bat and fuck off. Left him for dead—thought for sure I killed the bastard. But guess what? I find out later the cocksucker lived. Can you believe it? He lived."

Toby sat and swilled his beer, his face flushed.

"They are constantly finding new ways to get your money," Mac said. "Every time I think I know what they're up to, they invent something different."

"Tell me about it," Axel said. "Why, you got a new story?"

Mac nodded. "A few years ago when I was down here, a buddy of mine..."

Mac pointed to Sebastian Castillo, a mid-forties expat born in Switzerland, who had lived in the DR seven years. Mac considered Seb, a semi-retired corporate litigator, a friend; and a good one to have around these parts. Seb had cop connections as high up as the Colonel. At times, he paid them for protection. How much, Mac had no idea. And he didn't ask. If anything, he thought Seb's only mistake, something that might return to haunt him down the road, was getting a little too close to the cops. His live-in Dominican girlfriend Camila had begun to socialize with the Puerto Plata Sargent's wife. Even Seb had invited his cop connections out for drinks a few times. You get too close, too friendly, and the money extortion becomes more frequent and more costly. On a few occasions, the cops had given Seb a police escort home, three cops in a pick-up truck armed with M-16s following his vehicle, after a heavy night of partying in Puerto Plata. "You remember, Seb, you saved Pete's fucking ass."

Seb, at one time a suit-and-tie man who kept his brown hair short, had stepped out of the corporate fold and now conducted his legal practice at arms-length in beachwear, a full but neatly trimmed beard and long wavy hair.

"I did indeed, brother. Finish the story."

"I think you were there too," Mac said, pointing to Leonard.

"I don't remember, but maybe."

"You were there, old man," Seb said. "I know you were there."

"Whatever," Leonard said.

"Anyway, we're down on the Malecon, at the Rouge bar next to Raffi's. I'm shit-faced, with a buddy of mine from Nova Scotia, Marty Carbrera. This guy's a retired author, eccentric as hell. Last time he was here, he stayed in his apartment like a shut-in for most of the trip. I think he was too afraid of the culture to venture out. Anyhow, long story short, one night I finally get him out, and we're drunk at the Rouge. Some ugly Haitian hooker approaches Marty, grabs his shirt and starts pestering him, shit like that. I'm hitting on the hottie bartender at first so I don't notice what's happening. When I do notice her harassing him, I tell her nicely, the first time, to fuck off. After a while, she does. She returns a few minutes later and starts up with the harassment again. I'm pissed off by now, so I tell her angrily to get the fuck out of here. She does, returns five minutes later with two cops, their pick-up parked in the middle of the street, still idling. She explains to the cops that Marty stole her cell phone. I tell the cops 'no fucking way. This guy didn't steal her cell phone. He's down here for a two-week vacation, getting his teeth fixed.'"

Mac took a sip of beer and continued. "So the woman borrows a cell phone from a female accomplice, calls her number, and a phone in Marty's pocket starts glowing and ringing. He pulls it out, tells the cops he has no idea where it came from. The cops don't believe him and start escorting him out, saying they're taking him to jail. At this point I know I'm in over my head. I go around the corner to Raffi's, where Seb is drinking and yeah, I think you were there too Leonard. I tell Seb, 'I need your help, brother... the cops are taking my friend to jail...'"

"I remember it well," Seb said with a grin. "I told the cops he's a retired doctor with lots of money. He has no reason to steal a cell phone. They aren't buying my story until the dumb hooker starts yelling and screaming, pointing at Marty, saying, 'He's a criminal... take him to jail.' Then the cops start getting angry with this crazy cunt. One cop says, 'If you don't shut your mouth, I'm taking you to jail.' Anyway, I also started naming some of my higher-up contacts. The cops got a little nervous and released your friend."

"If it wasn't for you," Mac said, "I'm sure they would have hauled him off to jail."

"No doubt."

"I find out later the woman robbed Marty, picked his pocket of a hundred and fifty US cash. What he was doing with that amount of money down on the Malecon I have no idea. But he claims she stole it. The bitch plants a phone on him, robs him, and then tries to get him thrown in jail to extort more money out of him."

"I haven't heard of that kind of set-up before," Axel said. "She probably split the money with the cops."

"Could be," Seb said. "But there would have been a lot more to split had they hauled his ass to jail."

"What did your friend do after that?" Axel asked.

"Put his tail between his legs like a scared puppy and fucked off back to Canada," Mac said. "Can you believe it, the only time in two weeks I get him out for a drink and that shit happens?"

"Some people have no clue what they're doing here," Leonard said. "Fucking clowns."

The Swiss newbie, Swenson, who hadn't said a word, finally spoke. He looked like he was about to cry. "I was robbed last night."

"What?" Seb said, reaching for his phone. "Let's call the cops."

"Wait a fuckin minute... wait a fuckin minute," Leonard said. "Who robbed you?"

"A woman."

"What, some girl you brought back to your apartment?"

Swenson nodded.

"What did she take?" Mac asked. "Your computer? Money?"

A long pause. "No, my computer's safe. So is my money."

"You lose any credit cards, bank cards, anything like that?"

"No."

"Well, what the fuck did you lose, then?" Leonard asked.

"My mother's watch. She stole my mother's watch."

"Maybe you should file a report," Seb said. "If you have a description of this woman, I can assure you the cops will keep her out of Costambar. You may not get the watch back, but she won't bother you anymore."

Swenson nodded.

"What's her name?" Leonard said.

"Johanna."

"Not any of my regulars," Leonard assured him. "I remember names."

"I don't recognize the name," Mac said. Not that he would.

"You wouldn't know anyway," Leonard said. "Half the time you're too pissed to remember."

"Maybe so." There was much more to it than that, but Mac wasn't prepared right now to enlighten his audience. Once he left this motley crew, his first thought was to try and reach Maggie. But someone had to be told. The question was who and when? Who would believe him?

"Let me ask you a question," Leonard said to Swenson. "Besides the sentimental value, how much is this watch worth anyway?"

Another long pause.

Swenson's eyes were glazed and he looked zombie-like. "A hundred and fifty..."

"A hundred and fifty thousand pesos?" Leonard said. "That's a lot of money."

"No, fifteen hundred... fifteen hundred pesos."

"Fifteen hundred pesos... Are you fuckin kidding me? Are you fuckin serious, man? That's thirty-five dollars. That's a fucking thirty-five dollar watch." Leonard removed his stainless-steel wristwatch and handed it to Swenson. "Here, take this watch, for fuck sakes. That's all it's worth. Even less, actually. Take it and get over it."

Swenson did not extend his hand. He said nothing, still looked as if he would break down in tears at any second.

"That's not worth calling the cops about," Seb said.

"Fuckin right it's not," Leonard added.

A few minutes later, Swenson disappeared, saying he was going home to watch YouTube videos on his computer.

"Fuckin weirdo," Leonard said after he left.

"Never met him before," Mac said, "but he's a little strange."

"Just a little?" Leonard said.

"We're all strange," Seb said. "A bunch of lost souls. What do you think we're doing down here?"

"I know what you're doing down here," Leonard said with a smile. "Hiding from Interpol."

Seb smirked. "You keep that between this table. Hey, do you know there's a new police chief that just started working here?"

"No," Mac said. "I don't keep up with the cops."

"He shoots first and asks questions later," Seb said. "Just killed a burglar recently."

"We know him," Leonard said. "And I wish I knew him when those two hookers set us up."

"What happened?" Mac said.

Leonard explained the story. He and another friend Jonah had picked up two women, taken them back to their respective apartments, and proceeded to get busy. All of a sudden Jonah phones Leonard, telling him the women demanded more money and since Jonah wouldn't give it, stormed out in a huff. Getting nervous, Leonard kicked his woman out and went to Jonah's apartment. Soon the cops, with the two women, showed up. One woman claimed Jonah had a gun and had pointed it to her head. She also claimed he had fucked her with a knife. The cops couldn't find any gun, or bloody knife. But they hauled Jonah and Leonard off to jail for questioning. In the end, the cops weren't buying the hookers' story. None the less, Jonah and Leonard had to hire a lawyer before they were released from jail later that evening.

"If the stupid bitches hadn't have been so stupid about it, they could have gotten more money," Leonard said. "The cop says to the one girl, 'You got fucked with a knife did you? Pull down your pants and let's have a look.' Of course she wouldn't. But even still, we had to pay the cops, give the girls some money and pay a lawyer to get out of jail—one big fucking scam where the laws certainly don't favor the gringos. And everyone else gets paid."

"You have to watch the underage girl scams," Seb said. "Sometimes they'll go running to the cops, claiming you raped them. I know one guy who paid thirty thousand dollars—not pesos—to get out of jail, another one, a hundred thousand. Always ask for a cedula if you don't know them."

Andy Salise, a Canadian expat and long-time veteran of the DR, hadn't said much during the conversation. He owned a beachfront apartment building in Puerto Plata and had no interest in returning to Canada anytime soon. Swilling on a Cuba libre, he turned to Leonard: "The Dominicans sure do some stupid things sometimes."

Leonard only nodded.

"You should talk," Toby said, grinning. He turned to Mac. "Do you know this guy continues to see this Haitian woman who has already killed another woman? That's right, Niki stabbed a woman to death and Andy here goes and bails her out of jail. Now she's out walking the streets. That's gotta be the height of stupidity, never mind the Dominicans."

"I'm not seeing her anymore," Andy said.

"But, she's still out of jail and walking the streets isn't she?" Leonard said.

Andy nodded. "I know it was a stupid thing I did, but sometimes it's hard to see the forest for the trees down here. These women, they're master manipulators of men's heartstrings."

"A lot of Oscars have been won in the DR," Seb said.

"You got it," Andy said. "They're great actors. But I'll bet you they couldn't compete with us when it comes to matters of business or strategy."

"I doubt it," Seb said. "My girlfriend was university educated in Santiago, but she can't add 190 and 190. She knows it's less than 400 though."

Laughter around the table.

"I don't even find it funny anymore," Seb said. "I used to... but I've been with Camila for almost two years now."

"I like Camila," Leonard said. "She's got a big heart. She's a nice person."

"You want to trade," Seb said. "Or just take her."

"For now, I'll keep mine," Leonard said. "But I appreciate the offer."

Leonard had a two-year relationship with a statuesque, beautiful Dominican woman, called Stephanie, whose personality, smile and sense of humor never failed to light up a room. Her good looks and fine shape turned a lot of male heads and even female ones when she entered a room. Stephanie would disappear for a few days at a time. Leonard knew what she was up to, turning tricks, but the way he put it, "It's none of my fuckin business what she does in her spare time."

Leonard started to speak. He always had something to say. Just then, his phone rang. "Guess who?" he said. "Her ears must've been ringing."

He stood to take the call and walked a little ways from the conversation that was going up in volume, proportionate to the number of drinks being consumed.

Mac had been drifting during parts of the conversation. He didn't know if the gaps were in part due to his current level of intoxication, or more because of the nasty spell Maggie had inadvertently or intentionally placed on him. But the gaps were beginning to worry him. He found his mind drifting every time he looked at Michael, particularly at the claw-mark stretching from the bottom of his eye, across his cheek, and down to his nose. That was a nasty gash. And where did it come from? Finally, he said: "Where did you get that scar from?"

"Didn't you hear?" Seb said. "His ex-girlfriend attacked him on the beach with a stick. When she broke that over his head, her nails were the next best thing."

"Sorry about that," Mac said. "Where is she now?"

"Who?" Michael said.

"Your ex."

"Oh, Pamela. She fucked off."

"Didn't you call the cops or anything?"

"That's what I told him to do," Seb said, eyeing an attractive woman strolling past.

"No," Michael said. "She had every right. She caught me cheating on her."

"Hell hath no fury like a Dominican scorned," Axel said. Then to the waiter. "Get me another Cuba libre please. You want one Mac?"

Mac nodded.

"He claims he didn't cheat," Seb said, grinning like the Cheshire cat.

Michael's voice rose. "I didn't say that... I said I didn't remember cheating."

"Yeah, but you won't tell us why you didn't remember," Seb said.

Michael's eyes narrowed. "You wouldn't believe me if I did."

"Try me," Seb said.

Leonard had returned to his seat. He was all ears.

"I went to Maggie to get Pamela," Michael said. "She put a love spell on her. It worked for a while. You guys saw how crazy about me she was?"

A few heads nodded.

"What does it matter if you cheated?" Toby said. "How many of these Dominicans do you think are loyal? Not many, I'll tell you that. Hell, I bet my wife would cheat in a heartbeat given the opportunity. Her friend, her best friend I might add, fucked me the same day as she cut my wife's hair. She leaves my apartment building, meets me on the beach, and tells me she wants to do me. So, I do what any man would. I take her to a Cabana, rent a room for a few hours and pound the hell out of her. I'll tell you, man she was good. You know, that's my only weakness down here, besides booze, is pussy. My only weakness, pussy."

"I wanted to stay loyal, but one day I had this fucking blackout and got into trouble with other women," Michael said.

"That's what alcohol does," Leonard said. "Who is loyal down here anyway? What happens in Costambar, stays in Costambar. Look at all the married North American men coming down here and cheating on their wives. Their friends are around when they do it, fuck, the whole entire beach knows. But nobody says anything. In Canada, they might. But not here. Here, their moral codes become skewed or non-existent."

"No, this was more than just alcohol," Michael said. He explained what happened, as if they didn't know already, and finished the story by calling Maggie "a money-grubbing bitch whose love spells eventually turn nasty."

Mac couldn't help feeling the panic rise up from the pit of his stomach and assert itself with an acidy puke-like taste in his mouth. This denial had gone on long enough. While he wasn't up to telling this tough crowd his plight, for fear of being the laughing stock of the beach, he had to tell someone. Axel was a good person to start with. Tell Axel and get Axel to help him track down Maggie, who had yet to return two of his calls today. Get the fucking spell reversed and end this nightmare. Soon, he would have women beating him off with sticks on the beach for reasons he knew not, or could remember not.

"Anyway," Leonard said. "I have to go. Camila's meeting me at my apartment." He got up, paid his bill and left.

Mac took his cue. He touched Axel's arm and gave him that come-with-me-please look. "Why don't we go for a swim?"

Axel nodded. "Wait 'til I tell you about my session earlier."

They said goodbye, paid their bills, and rose to leave.

"Give me a call later," Seb said, as they departed. "If you want to get into some trouble on the Malecon let me know."

"Thanks, Seb," Mac said. "We'll see."

Chapter Seventeen

Livia could see things clearly now, she thought, leaving her apartment building for an afternoon stroll. Earlier, she had made a deal with Maggie. Maggie would erase Mac's recollection of their relationship, while it gave her time to plot his demise. Then, when he was taken care of, she could concentrate whole-heartedly on the emotional and financial ruination of Axel. She had made some strides earlier in the day with that agenda, during a heated sexual encounter, telling him how much she loved him, how gentle, passionate and caring he was; how his physical attributes impressed her. It was also his emotional intelligence, and his sensitivity to her needs. She had told him many things, spewed forth many terms of endearment. And she had noticed a subtle but encouraging change in his expression after the session ended. There was a look in his eyes, as if he was asking himself, "Is she the one?"

She reached a small convenience store where a number of Dominicans had already begun to party. A stereo outside blasted Merengue music, a few of them danced, and they all drank. Off to the side, a table and chairs were set up, where two men played Dominoes and others watched. Livia bought a loaf of bread, a bottle of rum and a bottle of Coke. Sure, she might be celebrating early, but what the hell. It was the Dominican Republic and the culture just lent itself perfectly well to getting hammered on a Monday afternoon. Over a few solitary drinks, she would plot the demise of Mac. It was a day to be happy, a day to end all days; a day to finally begin to see the end of the man who had insulted and offended her so many years ago.

Karma. It's a bitch. Just when you least expect it to, it bites you in the ass. She would make damn sure it bit Mac in the ass; it would ravage the hell out of it.

******

Violeta opened the door. At first, she had no idea what she was doing in Livia's apartment. She was still a little drunk from the earlier session with Mac. She had thought she had returned to Costambar that afternoon to track him down and see if he was willing to go another round with her. But that was silly, she thought, as a spark of lucidity entered her fuzzy mind. She vaguely remembered the night, but knew that when she left, the boys were none too pleased with her. What were the chances of Mac wanting to repeat a similar performance? *Zero to none.*

Then why was she here? *Because the door was open and you're a thief, that's why. You're not really a thief, just desperate for money right now is all.* Temporarily satisfied with that answer, she began searching the apartment. She went into the bedroom with a plastic bag and proceeded to fill it with jewelry. Underneath the mattress, she even found two thousand pesos, grinned, and stuffed it into her bra, out of eyeshot of her cleavage.

Realizing she was hungry, she went into the kitchen and opened the fridge. She pulled out a half-eaten piece of chicken and munched on it. After she had eaten, she went into the bathroom and closed the door.

******

I forgot to lock the door again, Livia thought, returning to her apartment. She went inside, set her groceries down and closed the door, locking two deadbolts and a handset lock.

She heard the toilet flush and froze, seized by raw fear. Adrenaline kicked in. She moved swiftly into the kitchen, fumbled in the cutlery tray, and removed a large butcher knife. She approached the bathroom door. "Who's in there?"

Livia moved a little too close to the door.

The door thrust open, smashing Livia in the face. She stumbled back and fell, the knife dislodging from her hand, flying across the room, bouncing off the apartment door and clattering to the floor. While she lay on the floor dazed, Violeta, with a bag full of stolen goods, ran to the door and tried frantically to open it.

Dazed, blood trickling from a cut on her forehead, Livia got to her feet.

Violeta, in her panic, couldn't figure out how to unlock the deadbolts. She put down her plastic bag, picked up the knife, and attacked Livia.

As Livia got up, Violeta kicked her square in the jaw. Livia emitted a painful squeal as she flew back, slammed into the wall and melted to the floor. Violeta renewed her attack. She kicked Livia twice more in the head, her pointed leather shoes opening a wide gash on her cheek, just below her eye. Blood squirted out.

Livia, screaming, began crawling along the floor.

Violeta knelt, raised the knife and plunged it at Livia's back. Livia rolled and the knife struck the ceramic tile and bounced out of Violeta's trembling hand.

Livia crawled toward it, but Violeta grabbed it first and plunged it down again. Livia grasped the blade. It slit a gash along the palm of her hand and more blood squirted out. But, she had a hold of Violeta's hands now.

A struggle ensued and they fought for control of the knife. They got to their feet and the struggle continued, as they gyrated around the room as though performing a bloodthirsty Voodoo ritual.

Livia staggered back and knocked over a lamp. It crashed to the floor, its ceramic base shattering everywhere. The bulb popped and fizzled.

Suddenly, Violeta jerked the knife free, pushed Livia onto the couch and dove on her. With one hand, she brought long nails down upon Livia's face, raking and drawing trails of blood. As Livia screamed and fought, Violeta raised the knife and plunged it deep into her throat. Livia screamed and dropped a hand to the floor, feeling around, knowing there was a pair of scissors there somewhere. She found them, brought her hand up and stabbed Violeta twice above the knee. Blood sprayed from the wounds, some of it landing on Livia's already blood-soaked face.

That's when voices could be heard outside the apartment, followed by pounding on the door. There was more than one voice. The other tenants had heard the commotion and rushed to Livia's aid.

"What the fuck's going on in there."

"Open up, or we'll kick the door in."

"Livia... are you in there? Are you all right?"

Frightened, Violeta dismounted Livia, picked up her plastic bag of stolen goodies, ran into the bedroom, smashed a second-floor window and jumped out. She hit the ground, twisting her ankle and winced in pain. Covered in blood, she limped along the narrow passage between two apartment buildings and escaped.

Upstairs, the concerned neighbors kicked the door open and entered. One was armed with a broomstick, the other a baseball bat and the third, a large dagger. What they found was a room covered in blood and Livia, lying on the couch, bleeding profusely.

"Quick," a tenant shouted. "Get your car started. We need to get her to a hospital."

Chapter Eighteen

It was a few days later, January 7th, that Mac first thought about going to the hospital. He had developed a rash on his bicep. Examining it in the mirror, he noticed it had spread to his chest. Not only that, the rash was forming red aggravated bumps, some of which were oozing smelly, putrid white puss.

Leaving the beach with Axel a few days earlier, he had begun absently scratching his bicep. To his horror, after they arrived at the pool, he noticed the rash had spread up his arm.

He still remembered Axel, swimming in the pool, looking at him curiously and asking, "Why aren't you coming in. The water's refreshing. It's so fuckin hot out."

Mac took a large swill of his Cuba libre—*that's the spirit, drown all your problems in alcohol, drink half the goddamned Brugal rum factory, why don't you*—and replied, "Not right now. Maybe later."

Instead, under the outdoor shower, he'd told Axel the whole story about Maggie and her love spell, starting from the very beginning. To Mac's surprise, Axel digested it with concern and belief. He did not laugh. He agreed to keep it confidential and help Mac get out of this mess. After a few drinks and three calls to Maggie went unanswered, they tried, to no avail, to find her at her business. The door was locked, the CLOSED, PLEASE COME AGAIN LATER sign dangling in the window.

Returning home after eating some pasta at a nearby restaurant, Axel met one of his regulars on the street and disappeared with her, telling Mac, "I'll call you when I'm done."

"It's okay," Mac said. "I'm just going to chill out for a change. I'll talk to you tomorrow."

He'd returned to his apartment, fretted about the rash for a few hours, became paranoid and started thinking that he was going to die soon. So he drank three more Cuba libres, popped two sleeping pills, and finally drifted off into a nightmare-filled and fitful sleep.

The next day he woke, drained of energy and listless. He had become even more paranoid and turned down a couple of offers to go to the beach for a drink. He didn't drink any alcohol that day and was convinced that he was going to suffer terribly and die a horrible death in the DR. For the time being, he had given up on contacting Maggie. He didn't go outside the entire day.

A phone call from Axel only fueled the fire of his paranoia. Axel was at Livia's bedside at the hospital. He told Mac of the attack on her life. The stab wound to Livia's neck had missed her jugular vein by a mere centimeter. That's how close to death she had come. A centimeter away. The attack had already horrified Mac, but when he learned Violeta, found limping on the beach a few hours later, had been arrested for the crime, he was paralyzed with fear.

And Axel's explanation of subsequent events didn't help matters: "I drove her to the hospital. Then I had to pay a lawyer twenty thousand pesos just to get Violeta arrested and thrown in prison. It turns out she's Haitian with no papers; an illegal in the DR. Anyway, the lawyer tells me that to prosecute her we're going to need his services. No such thing as a crown prosecutor down here apparently. And that'll cost more money and we might not even get a conviction. If I don't pay, they'll probably release her in a few days. And, who knows, I'm told she might charge Livia for stabbing her twice in the leg. Charge Livia for stabbing her in self-defense. I'll tell you something, brother, don't get into any legal shit down here, because the laws definitely favor the locals over the gringos—even if they're illegal. It's been two days and the cops haven't even investigated Livia's apartment. No crime scene tape or fuck all. I heard Toby's going to clean out all the blood if they don't plan on showing up."

After Axel hung up, Mac was left with a nagging feeling that he had a hard time shaking. A feeling that Axel might be in some kind of danger and Mac had the information that could help him. Only problem was, he couldn't retrieve that information from memory banks that lately seemed to be short-circuiting. There was, he thought, wincing at the nasty rash, throwing on a t-shirt and walking into the living room, one positive thing that had occurred over the last two days. He hadn't strayed from his apartment and slept with any hookers, nor had any of them come to his apartment. At least that's what his friends had confirmed anyway and there were no used condoms or empty rum bottles around the apartment to suggest otherwise.

That thought brought up two others—one, he still needed to contact Maggie, and two, he needed to get to a hospital or visit a doctor and get that nasty rash looked at. But, then something occurred to him. Maybe Maggie was the cause of the rash. Maybe she could cure it. At one time, Mac wouldn't have believed it. But this wasn't one time anymore. This was now and he had borne witness—hell, had been a human guinea pig—to the dark and mysterious power of her spells.

About to google skin rashes, Dominican Republic, he suddenly changed his mind and dialed Maggie. To his surprise, she answered on the first ring.

"Mac... listen I'm so sorry about not getting back to you. I've had some, well, family emergencies to deal with and it's required all my energy and—"

"Do you understand what kind of trouble I'm in? Let me tell you, I've been fucking my brains out around here lately and most of it I don't even remember. And, I don't know if this is your fault, but I'm drinking like a fish too. I'm—"

"I'm going to help you. Don't worry about a thing."

"I'm in serious trouble. Now I have a fucking rash that's oozing puss and I have no idea what it is."

"Meet me at my office at eleven tonight and I'll get you out of this. I promise."

Mac didn't realize how much stress he was under, but he could tell from his tone, it bordered on hysteria. "For fuck sakes, Maggie, what have you done to me? This is one fucking terrible nightmare."

"It's not entirely my fault. The dark spirits have been meddling with me."

Mac bit his tongue. He knew it would do no good to get angry and raise his voice. Maggie, he believed, held the key to a relatively normal life and he couldn't alienate her now, when he needed her the most. "And, you're sure you know how to fix this?"

"I'm pretty sure. Will you come at eleven?"

"I'll be there. What choice do I have?"

"Don't be late. It's important that you're on time."

She hung up the phone.

Mac reached for a cigarette, lit it and inhaled deeply, eyeing a half-full bottle of rum as if it were medicine. Maybe, at least for now, it was. He picked it up, noticing, not for the first time, his hand was trembling. Alcohol withdrawal symptoms, or fear for his life and condition, or maybe both, he knew not. But pouring a stiff drink, adding three ice cubes, and taking a deep swallow, he also realized he couldn't care less. He needed some tufts of fur from the wolves that had been ravaging him just to make it through the day.

He decided to stay in the apartment until it was time to meet Maggie. He would hole up alone with his fucked up psyche and nasty rash, have a few drinks and try and will himself to think more pleasant thoughts.

Three stiff drinks later, the only pleasant thought that popped into his head was the goddess-like image of Ophelia. So, in his infinite wisdom, he decided a drunk-dial to her was in order.

Chapter Nineteen

There was a certain order, Kalfu was now sure, a certain harmony to the events that had transpired recently. He had initially decided to possess Violeta to kill Livia. She was playing judge, jury and executioner with the spirit world after all and that was something that just wasn't permitted. In many ways, it was a crime befitting a death penalty. But, at the last second, he changed the lethal trajectory of the knife that plunged toward Livia's neck, changed it ever so slightly that he might spare her life.

Why?

It was simple, he thought, as he meditated in that dark and dank cave in the crossroads between the living and the dead. In many ways, Livia was a product of an abused upbringing and a mental disorder she had no control over. She did things impulsively to fit an agenda that involved revenge against men. Why? She had been victimized by her drunken father, verbally and physically abused and, one sordid night, damn near sexually abused. And the string of relationships shortly after she had matured into a beautiful woman was not much better. For the most part, she picked losers. And losers don't often treat women well. So, in her deranged mind, her agenda was completely justifiable. It was self-serving, but was also a form of protection and healing, a way she could cling to some semblance of sanity. After living a life of victimization and abuse, she took great pleasure in meting out what she viewed as revenge. It was like a rare fruit that once you tasted it, its sweet nectar would leave you wanting to devour more and more, growing into an insatiable appetite for vengeance

So, at the very last and fateful second, Kalfu had taken pity on her and spared her life. He thought maybe, just maybe, she was a candidate for redemption and reformation. As a powerful spirit of the crossroads between the living and the dead, it was part of his job, along with other Voodoo spirits, to make those decisions.

He stopped meditating for a second, took a deep swallow from the half-full bottle of rum, snuggled between his crossed legs, returned it to its position and continued to reflect on the master plan that was forming in his mind. He knew the Baron Samedi had been too busy attending other ceremonies of late to carry out his orders regarding the continued possession and eventual carnal destruction of Mac. But, he noticed, the Baron had cursed Mac with a nasty rash that, if left untreated, would send him to his death. So, that was good. In the absence of being able to fuck him to death, at least the Baron was taking other remedies to carry out his orders. But, therein lay the problem, Kalfu suddenly realized. Why was the Baron deviating from the order, why had he decided to execute Mac's demise in another fashion? Did the Baron have a plan of his own, perhaps a surreptitious agenda to undermine the great Kalfu's authority?

Kalfu wasn't sure, although he now suspected it to be so. Had the Baron decided on his own and without consultation from the other spirits that Mac also was a candidate for reformation and redemption? Was the rash merely an illusion of smoke and mirrors, a strategy to buy time while the Baron undermined Kalfu's orders? Kalfu needed to know. And if there was some validity to it, well then, he vowed in that instant to personally see to Mac's demise.

But, first, there was a much more pressing issue that needed his attention. The issue of Magdeline Ortega. She had been meddling with the spirit world for far too long now and her powers had become so strong that they could affect the behavior of the spirits and interfere with the natural order of the spirit world. And, if that wasn't enough, Kalfu had recently learned of her intention to become a spirit and thereby exact her revenge on him for the death of her father. Something had gone terribly wrong during the Voodoo ceremony that had resulted in Maggie's father's death. But Kalfu knew she would always blame him and always be vying for revenge. But during that fateful ceremony, he had been pulled in two different directions by the invasion of powerful and unknown evil forces. Although he was reticent to admit it, events had gotten out of his control. It was a mistake, although many Voodoo followers believed otherwise, to think that the spirits who provided positive guidance, healing, growth, happiness and love, were always in full control of a person's fate.

Like man, they were also subject to the forces of evil. Sometimes those forces could be controlled. Sometimes they couldn't.

Tonight was the night, Kalfu thought, taking a long pull on the bottle. As he resumed his meditation, a powerful thought started to form in his almost all-knowing mind. And, although he fought with all his will to prevent it from congealing, it did indeed rear its powerful and venomous serpent-like head. Was he, the great Kalfu, becoming possessed by evil forces beyond his control? Was this normal behavior for him to start plotting deaths?

He pushed the thought away and began a slow and melodic chant. He focused his all-seeing eye and slowly images materialized. Maggie was in a dimly lit room surrounded by glowing candles practicing witchcraft with three willing participants. It was time to carry out the master plan, time to insure that the power of the spirits would not now and would not ever be usurped by mere mortals. And, as he had thought earlier, there would be collateral damage.

But, collateral damage was the way the world was and would always be when it came to war.

Chapter Twenty

If Mac had any notion whatsoever that he might end up as collateral damage in some macabre plan to restore order in the spirit world, he certainly wasn't cognizant of it. He wasn't cognizant of much. He was certifiably hammered, he realized, as he sat around a table with Pamela, Michael and Maggie.

To his credit, however, he did ask why Michael and Pamela were a part of this ceremony which looked more like a séance than anything else.

"They inadvertently became a part of the last spell," Maggie said, averting her eyes slightly. "Somehow we angered the spirits and they got tangled up in all this. But... I'm... I'm going to fix it. Just be patient and do as I say."

Mac thought she was hiding something. And he was surprised to see Michael, particularly after he had trash-talked Maggie recently on the beach. Maggie must wield strong influence over her clients, Mac thought, as the thumping of drums began in the background, mixed in with some, presumably taped, ritualistic chanting.

The preamble was over. It was time for the ceremony.

"I want us to all join hands," Maggie said. "For this ceremony, I'm going to call in the Supreme God Bondye to set everything straight. It seems the other spirits have their own agenda."

It was too late to question anything, Mac, even in a highly inebriated state, realized. He opened his palms on the table. Maggie took his right palm, Michael his left, while Pamela, a look of mild annoyance on her small features, joined hands with Michael and Maggie.

"Now close your eyes," Maggie said. "This isn't going to hurt."

They did and soon Maggie began summoning the power of the supreme God. The drums beat and the background chanting continued, punctuating Maggie's words.

Through his alcoholic haze, Mac barely heard her invocations—"Bondye, Supreme Being, set this spell right so Michael and Pamela might find the love that has been eluding them, so that Mac might find the love that has been eluding him—"and then the words were lost in some impenetrable blackness that seemed to swallow all conscious thought.

Mac vaguely realized he might be passing out from none other than alcohol abuse but the thought was only fleeting. The blackness swept in and encompassed him, at least his mind. He still felt Maggie's soft dry hand on his right, Michael's twitching, clammy hand on his left. Mac didn't know if it twitched from fear or alcohol withdrawal.

Suddenly Mac lost control of his senses.

It was as if some powerful deity had high-jacked the ceremony. He no longer felt the hands; those of the others or his own. He was rocketed down a spiraling dark tunnel. He heard the horrible screams of the damned before slithering through blood-soaked bodies, joined together in some hellish carnal union, cackling and screaming, cackling and screaming, joy intermingled with pain.

His heartbeat quickened. He closed his eyes tighter and fought for something to hang onto. He willed his mind to bring him out of this horror and tried to summon feeling in his extremities. It took some time and more slithering around in blood-soaked debauchery before he felt it. Yes, it was Maggie's hand and he was still holding it.

It gave him faint hope, although it felt like all his will, all his strength, was being sapped. He willed his brain to find the feeling in his left hand, wanting to know if Michael was still there. But, when he squeezed, all he felt was air.

Then the evil forces took full-throttle control over the ceremony.

He heard a terrible scream in his right ear, felt Maggie's hand jerk free, another high-pitched painful scream and a loud crash. He willed his eyes to open.

They would not.

Another crash, another scream.

Finally, Mac's eyes did open. And what he saw was so frightening it might have been edited from the original version of The Exorcist. Maggie's body was in the corner of the room, convulsing spasmodically. Her eyes were wide open but the pupils had retreated into her head and only the whites were visible. As she twitched, some invisible force slammed her repeatedly into the wall. With each painful blow, blood sprayed on the walls and around the room.

Pamela's head was slumped on the table, unconscious.

Or dead.

Michael stood at the door, his unsteady hand gripping the light switch. He had risen at some point and switched it on. His eyes were wide, his mouth agape. He watched the carnage unfold and said nothing, frozen and locked into the horrific moment.

An adrenaline boost with a remarkably sobering effect charged through Mac and he found his legs. He stood, took a few steps, grabbed Maggie's dangling leg and began yanking, trying to free her from the torture that was killing her.

Chapter Twenty-One

"You kill me, falling for that shit," Seb said.

He took a swallow from his Cuba libre, watched and waited for Axel's reaction, as they sat in a beach bar on the Malecon. It was midnight and they had no idea that, just a few miles away, Mac was involved in a terrifying life and death struggle.

Axel, for his part, had just told Seb he thought Livia was changing her ways after her near-death encounter with Violeta. After leaving Livia's hospital bedside earlier, Axel, unable to reach Mac, had met with Seb and Leonard for a few drinks on the beach. As is often the case, this led to a trip to the Malecon for a few more.

When Seb heard of the attack on Livia, while sympathetic, he was quick to fill Axel in on the nature of Livia's true character, saying, "She will chew you up into little pieces and spit you into the garbage."

"No, I really think this time is different. She's different."

"She's a manipulator and that's part of her plan."

"I've seen that woman go through more fucking men than Seb can drink Cuba libres," Leonard said, pouring himself another drink from a bottle of white rum. "Why do you bother with a North American woman anyway, when you can have almost any one of these young hot Dominicans?"

"I think culturally, I have a lot better chance of finding more in common with a woman from the first world," Axel said, flashbacks of the night with Violeta popping into his head. "I mean, unless you want to live here permanently, try and bring a Dominican back to Canada. Do you think they'll like our winters, our culture?"

"No, I don't think they would," Seb said, eyeing a table of four attractive Dominican woman, who were looking right back. "But, it's the variety that keeps me living here. I mean, the women back home would hardly give me the time of day. It's so tempting, very difficult to stay monogamous. And I have a nice Dominican girlfriend, who, overall, treats me well. I don't even know why she stays with me, all the fucking around I do."

"She knows where her next meal is coming from," Leonard said. "But I like Camila. She's a nice girl."

"Where's your girlfriend?" Axel asked.

"Probably turning tricks somewhere," Leonard said matter-of-factly. "I don't care."

"The thing is it's so easy to meet women down here," Seb said. "I've been living down here many years and fucking around. All I'm doing is playing the game and trying not to push it too hard, trying to stay away from the ones whose bad intentions you can almost sense."

"They all wanna fuck with you. Every time I turn around someone is trying to fuck with me," Leonard said.

"I think I've heard that before," Axel said.

"He repeats himself a lot," Seb said. "It's the alcohol. Do you know, if I drank this much back home, I would be encouraged to join Alcoholics Anonymous. Here, I would have to join a group called Anti-Alcoholics Anonymous. Foreigners on the island are almost ashamed to say publicly 'I'm not drinking at all.'"

"I don't need to go out and have a drink," Leonard said. "But I like to have a drink. And if I was in Canada I'd be bored as shit in no time. I'd rather be bored here."

"I don't think you're bored here," Seb said. "Let me finish my story. Maybe they do have an AA here but I guarantee you it would be something that would be underground... which brings me to my main point. You know, in a few weeks I have to return home to take care of some business stuff. It might take me three months. I haven't been back for three months in eight years. Do you know what kind of shock therapy that would be?"

"Maybe you'll find yourself again?" Axel said.

"When I leave this whore-dancing-bitch-ass-slapping-rum-drinking island I'll find myself in an environment I can hardly remember. And that will for sure not be the same. It'll be like a clinic where they put the alcoholics where they would pay a hundred dollars to buy a drink from somewhere. Where you find out your own Mr. Johnson is mad at you because he didn't realize how spoiled he was before and finds himself in a weird environment where ladies don't pay much attention to him..."

"What's wrong," Leonard said. "You forgot what you were saying?"

"No. I was finished. I was just thinking about what Axel said. Maybe you're right. Maybe my time back home in quietude and silence will be a good test for me. Maybe it'll be a meditative road back to finding myself..."

Seb's voice trailed off again, as one woman from the table of four winked, smiled, and waved him over. He stood up. "But there will be time enough for that. Why am I being so damn philosophical anyway? I'm here now, aren't I?"

He approached the table and sat down with the ladies.

"He can't keep his dick in his pants," Leonard said with a grin. He turned to Axel. "Hey, you heard from Mac today?"

"Talked to him earlier," Axel said. "Called him after that but he doesn't answer."

"He's probably got his dick caught in some hole too."

"I don't know. I'm gonna call him now... maybe he'll want to join us with those four?"

"I thought you said you were getting interested in Livia?"

"I am... but I'm here now, aren't I? May as well make the best of it."

Chapter Twenty-Two

Waking to the vile stench of urine and decomposing human feces, Mac's best guess was he had been in hot dark captivity for a week; lying on a dirt floor of a tin-roofed shack somewhere in the countryside. Yes, a week seemed right. He had begun marking the days. Clad only in dirty and shredded travel shorts, ankles and wrists tightly bound with rope, he had gripped a twig between his toes and used it to scratch the days off. Each morning the roosters would cock-a-doodle-doo and each morning Mac would scratch another line in the dirt, marking the beginning of another dreadful day.

The man who visited him every day was called Fractus Menses. He would see to it that Mac was fed and watered and led to a small hole in the corner of the room to relieve himself. Fractus would also tell Mac every day before leaving, "Don't worry, your time is coming. Soon you have freedom."

Mac didn't know what the word freedom meant to Fractus. He suddenly heard the dissonant high-pitched rooster calls and, noticing a single line of sunshine stray into the blackness from a crack in a misshapen wooden wall board, he grimaced and scratched another jagged line into the dirt. Seven lines, one week. And he wondered if freedom would mean the same gruesome death that Maggie had suffered.

During the ceremony that had gone terribly wrong, Michael had snatched up Pamela, the only possession that mattered to him, and like some heroic firefighter rescuing a blaze victim, fled the building carrying her, leaving Mac struggling to try and save Maggie's life.

But Mac's efforts had been futile, he remembered. Getting splattered with droplets of Maggie's spraying blood, he had pulled with all his strength before finally jolting her free from the invisible and powerful torture. They landed together on the floor with a loud thud, Maggie on top, in his arms. There was a moment of recognition in her fearful eyes. The black pupils returned from their sojourn inside her head and locked with his. She had shouted, "Help me, pleeeeease!"

And Mac had gotten her to her feet and began helping her to the door. But a few feet away, the powerful evil force seized her and flung her into a wall where a large spear magically appeared. As she struck the wall, the spear impaled her heart. He watched, horrified, as the life drained from her eyes. Her head slumped to one side and blood gushed from her mouth and she died. Unable to stomach the image, Mac had closed his eyes, just for a second, but long enough for someone to burst through the door and knock him unconscious with a blunt instrument. When he woke, Mac didn't know how much time had passed. He was blindfolded, bound and gagged, in the back seat of a vehicle, as it bounced along a bumpy road.

He heard two men talking in the front seat but, muzzy-headed from the alcohol and concussion, understood only snippets of the Spanish conversation.

"Fractus will be pleased. Look, he's not dead. He's waking up. We can't kill him. Fractus gave us specific instructions. He wants him alive—as healthy as possible. This will be a great day. Our people will be saved."

Listening to the roosters crow, Mac twisted, turned and rolled over so he might get a better view through the tiny crack that had recently appeared. He inched closer to the opening and peered out. There was a small clearing with a large mass of tree branches piled high in a burn pit, dense foliage and the indigenous trees of the countryside. He listened for other sounds. Dogs barking, somewhere a baby crying, birds chirping, the faint din of conversation, some distance away. But no vehicle sounds. This was definitely the countryside. But where?

He rolled over and surveyed his surroundings. He did not want Fractus to see him looking outside, lest he suffer his wrath. The room was very dark and it took some time before his eyes could adjust after peering directly into bright sunlight. Slowly the room came into view. Wooden boards haphazardly hammered together made up the inside. A dirt floor with a few rocks, a tin roof and a single white blanket in a corner, spotted with dirt stains; his bed he presumed.

He inched his way to the bed, sighed heavily and rolled over onto his back, trying to get in tune with his physical condition. He felt something caked on his forehead and assumed it was dried blood from the blunt force trauma he had suffered earlier. He looked down at his ankles, bound tightly with ropes, and noticed more dried blood. He studied his wrists, tied in front of him with ropes. More dried blood and a painful itching sensation, which, after waking this morning from a sweat and nightmare-filled sleep, he had refused to acknowledge. But now, eyes widening with horror, he realized it was the rash. It had spread down both arms, onto his hands, chest and stomach. And the nasty pustules were still there, oozing and spreading what Mac was now sure was certain death.

He lay there for a long while, trying to squash the seedling of fear with his will. But soon, it sprouted and grew, spreading its poison-ivy tentacles throughout his entire body. He convulsed as it possessed him. Spittle dribbled down his mouth. After a few moments, some giddy emotion bordering on madness replaced the fear and he cried out: "God, if you really exist, get me out of this... please."

His voice echoed hollowly in the ramshackle shack and he lay for a few minutes staring at the ceiling, a lone tear forming and glistening on his left eye. He winced, closed his eyes, and it rolled down his cheek, dangling on his upper lip. He rolled his tongue across his mouth, tasted the salty drop and tongued his lips with it. That brought another thought, another craving.

"Okay, God... you're not here. So fuck you anyway. If I'm going to die grant me three wishes. Give me a fucking smoke, a drink, and a beautiful woman to fuck. For fuck sakes, give a dying man his wishes, will you?"

A few minutes passed. Nothing happened. Mac closed his eyes and remained silent for a long while. Finally, he opened them.

The image of Ophelia suddenly formed above his head, fragmented at first, but then all the tiny pieces of the puzzle joined and her large, beautiful face looked down on him with deep concern. Her hair was long, blonde and flowing, just as he remembered it; her eyes a deep and mesmerizing chestnut-brown; her lips, succulent and her smile bright.

"Is that you, Ophelia?"

The image disappeared in an instant. Then there was only the small stray line of sunshine and the darkness in his mind.

And Mac remembered. He had drunk-dialed her prior to leaving for Maggie's. What had he said? Was she happy to hear from him? Fragmented and disjointed thoughts crystallized into a vague memory. Yes, he had told her he was in deep trouble. Said he wasn't responsible for his behavior in PEI, but everything was going to be better now. That's right—everything's going to be better. He had explained the entire story to her about the botched love potion and the after events, everything... albeit slightly abridged. After the explanation, there was a long silence on the other end of the line and finally Ophelia said: "All I can say is for your part, I hope you sort it out and get back to Canada in one piece." And one more thing, before hanging up. "Please don't call me when you're drunk. I don't know what to believe and what not to believe anymore with you. But, you've got a problem with booze and women and you need to fix it."

"But, I'm going to... I'm going to. Listen Ophelia, I need to tell you..."

But she was gone. He remembered it now. He had heard the line click dead.

What had he been thinking? Drunk-dialing the only woman he thought was his soulmate. *Soulmate? You hardly know her you idiot.*

But he wanted to think more about her. In his misery, it was the only thing that brought him some measure of peace. He began to think of their first date, how giddy with excitement being with her made him feel.

But, before he could realize any joy from the memory, a wooden door creaked open. The bright sunlight blinded Mac. He closed his eyes.

The door closed part way.

He opened his eyes, squinting.

At first the man standing in front of him was shrouded in blackness. Then slowly his features came into view. He was Haitian: tall, slim, pointed nose, a wide smile with crooked teeth and black, soulless eyes. An S-shaped scar on his cheek added to the menace. He wore a white loin cloth and a black bandanna was wrapped around his head, concealing most of his short black curly hair.

He sat cross-legged in front of Mac.

"Here," he said, putting a water bottle to Mac's lips. "Drink, for tonight is your night."

Mac slowly sat up, leaning his back against the wooden wall. He opened his mouth, which was parched and lined with dust. Fractus poured and Mac swallowed six mouthfuls before choking on the seventh and spitting most of it out. It dribbled down his cheek.

Fractus lifted a wooden bowl with some rice and began to spoon-feed Mac. He ate six mouthfuls, chewing and swallowing slowly before closing his mouth and shaking his head. "I've had enough. When are you going to let me out of here?" Glancing at his spreading rash, he added, "Can't you see I'm dying?"

Fractus shook his head and grinned. "No, no, no... you're not dying. You're about to be reborn."

Along with the fear and the irrational thoughts, pushing the boundaries of sanity, there was something else boiling up inside Mac. Anger. He tightened his facial muscles, narrowed his eyes and aimed the green daggers at Fractus. "When I get out of this you skinny little shit, I'm going to make you wish you were never born. I don't know what you're planning to do with me, but I know it isn't good. So, when I get out of this... I'M GOING TO FUCKING KILL YOU!"

Fractus switched to a kneeling position and slapped Mac hard in the face.

Mac spit in his eye.

Fractus wiped it away with a grin.

"Fuck you, you Voodoo freak. You ever heard of such a thing as karma... I guess not, eh? Probably not part of your crazy religion. Karma's a bitch when it cuts your fucking head off." Mac realized after he had said it that, in his rage, he had switched from Spanish to English. Most of the dialogue he'd had with Fractus to this point had been in Spanish.

Fractus cocked the wooden bowl.

Mac closed his eyes and felt two sharp hollow knocks on his head, a third connecting brutally with his mouth and slicing his upper lip open. He licked the wound, tasting the acidity copper flavor of blood. Up to this point, he hadn't given Fractus this much grief. He had tried to be a diplomat; mistakenly thinking he could win his favor and perhaps escape what he now fully realized was going to be a death sentence. But, it was no use. This morning, everything became clear with dreaded certainty. It was the rash. It was the fear. It was the anger. It was the alcohol, tobacco and hooker withdrawal. It was the poisonous jaws of insanity, snapping at a tumultuous mind. It was the unrequited love for Ophelia. It was utter hopelessness and despair and it could not, would not, be contained.

He continued speaking in English. "The light's on but nobody's home. Knock all you want, you won't find the

Macburger. Where's the beef, Fractus? Or should I call you Fucktus, or maybe just plain old fashioned fuck up..."

Fractus frowned, turned and left.

Mac burst into hysterical, giddy laughter. His eyes were wild and wide. Blood from the cut lip drained down his chin, giving him the appearance of a crazy, blood-frothing wild wolf.

If the time was now, he was going to handle it the only way he knew how—like a raving nutcase.

Chapter Twenty-Three

And that evening, as frenzied naked women chanted and gyrated around a blazing fire, drummers pounded out a frenetic rhythm, and Fractus, cross-legged, composed and serene, shook the snake vertebrae rattle and hummed, Mac, arms and legs tied on a nearby cross, thought for sure he had gone nuts. The realization of his end had finally fully arrived at the door to his senses. It had knocked. It had entered. It had terrified him.

And he thought it had driven him nuts.

So, like any nutcase, he laughed hysterically at the notion of his own death. But, before he could drop into the abyss of complete insanity, he reached out and, with a straying hand, snatched at some semblance of logic in a decaying mind. *Wait a minute. Am I really going to die? Maybe Fractus was right? Maybe I've found my freedom.*

Before Mac could give it much thought, a little girl in a dirty white tattered dress was led in front of the fire. With crazed eyes, he watched as she struggled with two men holding her wrists. She screamed and flailed her arms to no avail. She looked stark raving mad.

They placed her in front of the fire and forced her to sit. She continued screaming and darting her eyes around the congregants, as if searching for a savior.

Fractus stopped humming. "Quiet, my child. You will be healed."

With that, she shut her mouth, sat quietly, and the men left her alone. The frenzied women, who had stopped dancing, resumed their frenetic undulations around the fire. The drumbeat quickened and Fractus began an incomprehensible chant.

An invocation to the spirits to cure this girl, thought Mac.

Two men led a goat through the throngs of onlookers and worshippers. They wrestled it to the ground, beside the little girl. Knowing it was going to its death, it squawked horribly, kicking and bucking frantically. The men finally got control of its legs and held it down securely. One raised a large dagger, uttered some high-pitched cry, lowered it, and expertly slit the goat's throat. It squealed dreadfully as it died. As blood sprayed out, a man cupped his hands underneath, while others gathered around with wooden bowls to capture the dark red liquid. They drank from the bowls.

Fractus stopped shaking the rattle. He stood and approached the little girl. Two men, wooden bowls filled with blood, began pouring it on the girl and wiping it all over her body.

She sat serenely, as if transfixed in a powerful spell.

Fractus spread his arms to the sky and spoke: "I call to you, great Kalfu to cure the madness within Katrina, heal her mind and make her sane again."

A wind whipped up and a mini-tornado circled the blaze.

Fractus continued: "The spirits have been angry lately. Humans have meddled with their powers and they seek vengeance." He pointed to Mac. "We must sacrifice this man here for daring to tamper with the spirit world. Kalfu has given the order and it must be carried out. It is then that Kalfu, the great spirit of the crossroads, will decide if this man is worthy of leaving our world and passing permanently into a life of torture or joy in the spirit world."

Four natives, clad in loin-cloths, approached the cross, lifted it, carried it in front of the flames and rested it on a large nearby boulder, a few feet from Katrina.

The chanting continued.

The drumbeat quickened.

A blood curse, Mac thought. *This is a fucking blood curse.* "Get me out of this torture," he shouted. "I don't care anymore. Finish it, will you?"

So close to death, the fear evaporated. The terror, even the bulldozer of lunacy, for the moment parked itself in a vacant but secured parking lot somewhere deep in the recesses of his mind. So near to death, people react in very different ways. Some go quietly, some panic, others get angry, some go nuts, some apologize for their sins, still others cry like little babies. Mac had felt all of these emotions, but now he felt only resignation. Finally the suffering would end, and he was almost glad for it. *What have I done, anyway? A self-serving life of debauchery and sin. Fucking, drinking, fucking and drinking. Let it all end. If there is a God, these motherfuckers will get their just desserts...*

A native wielding a blood-soaked dagger approached, lowering it to Mac's throat.

Suddenly Katrina's head turned. Her intent eyes focused on Mac.

"No," she shouted, standing up. "You can't die, you can't kill him. It's not his time." Before anyone could stop her, she raced to Mac, rested her bloodied head on his bare chest and hugged him tightly, shouting, "No, no, not Mac, it's not his time..."

Fractus waved a hand and immediately two natives began pulling Katrina off. She held on tightly and they struggled with her new-found force.

"Kill her," Fractus ordered. "Something's wrong."

A dagger-wielding native approached, wrapped an arm roughly around her head and yanked her back.

"Kill them both," Fractus demanded. "Kill them now."

The native brought the dagger to her throat.

Another native brought a dagger to Mac's throat.

Mac felt warm steel touch his throat. As the dagger penetrated skin, he felt a burst of sharp pain and hot blood pour down his chest. He didn't know how much of it was his, how much Katrina's, but he knew the suffering would soon be over.

He smiled, closed his eyes, slumped his head to one side and succumbed to the black void. *That's it, that's all* was the last thought that went through his mind.

"Now," someone shouted from the cover of the forest.

A shot rang out and a bullet smashed through the head of the native sacrificing Mac. He slumped on Mac's chest.

Another shot rang out and shattered the skull of Katrina's attacker. He lurched back, uttered a loud guttural moan, staggered into the blazing fire, fell into it and instantly burst into flames.

Mass pandemonium ensued. The drums stopped beating, people screamed and fled into the forest.

Fractus bent down, picked up a fallen dagger and approached Mac. He examined the large gash on Mac's neck, the copious amounts of draining blood, and decided he too was quite dead. But he didn't want to take any chances. He raised the dagger high in the air with both hands and readied to plunge it deep into Mac's heart.

A soldier emerged from the forest, stopped six feet from Fractus, and pointed an M-16 at his head. "Stop or I kill you."

"I'm dead anyway. The spirits will take their revenge."

As he began to thrust the blade, the soldier riddled him with bullets. A stray bullet blasted the dagger out of his hand, but ricocheted back and struck the soldier between the eyes, killing him instantly. Fractus fell on Mac's bloodied chest and proclaimed, "The spirits will avenge."

Fractus spewed forth a fountain of blood from his agape mouth, groaned loudly, and died.

Chapter Twenty-Four

I'd die to get into her pants, Axel thought, as he watched a shapely bikini-clad Haitian strolling along Costambar beach. *I love her shapes... curves in all the right places.* For a rare change, he sat by himself at a beach bar that Friday afternoon, January 31st, sipping what had become his drink of choice—Cuba libre. Sure it was only eleven-thirty in the morning, but it was definitely past noon somewhere in the world. *May as well get started early.*

The meandering woman stopped at the water and bent down, giving Axel ample view of her tantalizing cleavage. She picked up a pebble, winked, smiled and tossed it into the water. She spun around and seductively curled a finger at Axel. Come here and fuck me, she seemed to be saying.

"Maybe a little later," Axel said.

"I'll be back," she said, spinning around and strolling away.

He took another sip, admiring the way her beautiful buttocks bounced as she walked, wondering if local women did that deliberately to lure men in, or was that just how they moved? He let the thought evaporate. He had other things to think about right now and wanted to clear his head with a few more drinks so he could concentrate.

The hot sun warmed him. He contemplated his life here. Livia had been released from the hospital two weeks ago and was trying to turn over a new leaf. For a while, things had been good between them. Livia, for the first time in her life, had confessed her agenda to Axel, but said she didn't want to be that person anymore. She wanted to be different, loyal and honest, with no secret agenda to ruin men. The near-death experience, she claimed, had been life-changing. A way for her to realize the destructive path she was on, a way for her to try and rectify it while there was still time.

Maggie's death had also reinforced that point. "You mess with the spirits, drive on the wrong side of the moral highway, and you're in danger of getting seriously injured or killed," Livia had said.

Axel had believed her. And for his part, he too had tried to change. Things went well for about a week until they learned Violeta had been released from jail and was considering pressing charges against Livia for attempted murder. The only way to send her back to prison to face charges was to pay a lawyer. Axel didn't have the money for that and Livia thought it was a lost cause. There was no guarantee of success. This news sent them both into a funk, coming to the realization that, for foreigners, there is often no justice in the Dominican Republic.

Livia handled the stress by taking a handful of pills, drinking two bottles of vodka and almost killing herself.

Axel handled the news by buying a day-pass at a five-star resort, drinking himself into blackout mode, picking up two hookers on the Malecon, bringing them back to his apartment and fucking their brains out all night.

Costambar is a small community. It's not easy to keep secrets. Everyone knows or wants to know what you're up to. Oftentimes, they know what you did last night even before you remember, if you do at all. Axel was spotted with the hookers and news got back to Livia.

She promptly met a gringo tourist on the beach, lured him back to her apartment and fucked his brains out. A very simple motive—revenge.

After that, everything fell apart. Livia went back to her mission to ruin men emotionally and financially and Axel returned to his wild womanizing and drinking ways. Only this time, the blackouts were getting worse along with his selection of women. Oftentimes, he was spotted in the seediest barrios of Puerto Plata, pissed out of his mind, picking up the most unattractive and untrustworthy of hookers. Twice he had been robbed of small amounts of money and once he had almost landed himself in jail after an underage hooker set him up and then claimed he had raped her. Fortunately for Axel he was a friend of Seb.

It had been Seb's police connections that led to a ten-thousand peso bribe; a get-out-of-jail-not-so-free card.

People were beginning to talk. "Axel doesn't remember anything when he drinks...It's a complete blackout...One of these days he's going to get himself killed... He better watch himself, I'll tell you that much... You see that hooker he was with the other night? She looked like Jabba the Hutt... she jumps in the hot tub in a Cabana with him and it's like a tsunami wave. Her pussy's so big I could park my truck in there... he's become addicted to sex and alcohol."

Ordering two more drinks, on some level, Axel realized if he continued along this path he might eventually wind up dead. And there was something else bothering him. He thought he really had a chance of a decent relationship with Livia and maybe, just maybe, he was even in love with her. But, that train of thought quickly derailed, flew off the tracks of cognitive thinking and shattered into a million pieces.

Now, he had no idea how to repair it.

Loading a jumble of thoughts and regrets into a brand new train of reconciliation, he imagined smoke puffing from its chimney, even heard a little choo-choo-choo blast from its horn, and watched it chug-chug-chug on the rails and up a steep mountain. *Oh, to get the top of it, to get over that mountain without getting derailed again, how sweet it would be. How sweet, how sweet, how...*

For a long time, Axel got lost in thoughts of a new life, a new beginning. But, when the Haitian beach-walking beauty sauntered up to his table with an attractive smile and an eager friend in tow, those thoughts vanished completely, like puffy white exhaust clouds from a steam engine train.

"Hi, I'm Jiedy. This is my friend Mindy. Do you mind if we sit down?"

Axel grinned. "I'm Axel and be my guest."

As the conversation started, Axel's phone rang. He looked at the number and smiled widely. He answered it. "Mac, how you doing, bro?"

"I thought you were coming at eleven," Mac said.

"Sorry, I forgot. But, I'm on my way. And I've got a surprise for you. We're going to have a recovery party."

Chapter Twenty-Five

Recovering in hospital after his near-death experience, Mac had had a lot of time for introspection. Now, sitting on a bench outside the hospital, watching pedestrians and motoconchos come and go, he realized if Axel hadn't called him that night at Maggie's ceremony he would indeed be dead. He was lucky to have friends like Axel, luckier still to have friends like Sebastian. Before Mac was knocked unconscious, he'd had the foresight to tell Axel, "If I go missing, please try and find me."

It was that plea that had led—through Seb's connections—to a military search-and-rescue operation; one that had eventually saved Mac's life. Sure, it had cost him a thousand dollars. The cops and military don't rescue gringos for free. But, what was a life worth anyway? And, for that fee they had agreed to keep everything hush. They had their own motives for keeping it quiet anyway. It wouldn't do tourism much good if foreigners learned about his near-death experience at the hands of a Voodoo priest who had strayed well into the dark side of the strange and mysterious religion. No, tourists wouldn't be encouraged to visit the DR if they learned Mac was being used as a human sacrifice in some bizarre ritual to appease angry spirits.

And the nasty rash, that Mac had become convinced was the work of angry spirits, was actually a rare but curable fungal infection. In the hospital, doctors had treated him with antibiotics, a topical cream and a special anti-bacterial soap. In eight days, the rash had disappeared, although he still bore a few scars.

He also had a two-inch scar above his right eye from the initial blunt force trauma when he was first kidnapped. And his throat bore a four-inch scar where the dagger-wielding man had tried to kill him. It had missed his jugular vein by one centimeter. He, like Livia, had come a centimeter away from death.

Surprisingly, she was one of the visitors who had come to his bedside to offer him moral support. As well as Sebastian, Leonard and Axel, Livia also arrived at the hospital by herself one day. And, in a moment of lucidity, Mac had recognized her. It was a tear-jerker moment. He had been about to order her out of the room, when, perched sorrowfully on a bedside chair, she had grasped his hand tightly, tears welling up in her sad eyes, and said: "I'm so sorry for the way I treated you all those years ago. I know I have many problems and I'm trying to fix them. I had no right saying those things to you. My only hope is that we can be friends. I hope you can find it in your heart to forgive me."

Seeing the emotion and sincerity in her eyes, he had wilted and agreed to try and be her friend and even help her on the road to recovery and rehabilitation.

Help her. He lit a smoke and inhaled deeply. *I don't know if I can even help myself.*

Mac was still mystified by some of the events. He was still haunted by Maggie's violent death—that too had been hushed up to some degree and attributed to a robbery gone bad. He wondered, with Maggie gone, was he cured of the deleterious spell? Would he return to blackout periods with multiple hookers, driven by some unseen and unknown force?

Or had the little girl—Katrina, that was her name—who suddenly clung to him while he was on his sacrificial death bed somehow reversed the spell and saved his life? He knew, while in the hospital, he hadn't strayed. Nurses, doctors and friends had confirmed it. But now that he had recovered, would he go back to his debauched ways? He hoped against all hope he would not. He had initially planned on taking the first plane back to PEI as soon as he was released. But some unknown force seemed to be keeping him here. After waking from a terrible nightmare involving Katrina's gory sacrificial death, he had decided to extend his stay. He had changed his return date to April 26th. There were just too many unanswered questions he needed answers to.

First and foremost among those, was the question of his own physical and mental health. During recovery, the poisonous tentacles of insanity had not returned. But did that mean they wouldn't? And what would happen to him upon his return to PEI? Would he be, as the police had said, inappropriately touching young girls on the street? Had one of these girls, as the cops had indicated, decided to press charges for sexual assault? Was he a wanted man in Canada now, like so many others hiding out in the DR?

He wanted to believe he was cured. He wanted to believe he could walk a higher moral ground. He had vowed, during his recovery, to turn over a new leaf. But could he do it? Was the temptation too great, were the effects of the curse still there, waiting for the right time to rear their demonic heads?

He finished his smoke, stubbed it out on the side of a garbage can and tossed it inside. There would be time to think about that later. His ride was here.

Axel pulled curbside, smiled and waved. Two attractive women sat in the back, smiling as Mac approached.

This'll be the test. He climbed in, shook Axel's hand, thanked him and ogled the female passengers.

"I brought you a surprise," Axel said, sipping a drink and pulling away from the curb. "Which one do you want, bro? Or, do you want both? Doesn't matter to me. It's your coming-home party."

Mac looked at the women and introduced himself.

Jeidy smiled, unstrapped a medium-sized perfectly shaped breast and massaged her nipple. It stiffened.

That wasn't the only thing that stiffened. All of Mac's resolutions vanished in an instant. "I'll take Jeidy, and I need a drink... badly."

As they drove and Axel brought him up to speed on local news, or gossip depending on your perspective, Mac tried hard to will the flagpole to half-mast. But, like a true patriot, it stood proud, ready, willing and eager to perform its carnal duty.

Try, try again, Mac thought with a smile. *Try, try again*.

Chapter Twenty-Six

As it so often does, time passed quickly—and Mac tried to put the train on the right track. That evening—two months ago—leaving the hospital, he of course had succumbed to the tempting fruits of Jeidy's body. And he had feasted on them. She had performed admirably—hell, she was a devil in disguise in bed. He had paid her, there had been no drama, and she had left. But, in the days to follow he had tried to steer a more righteous path.

Although Ophelia's ghostly image still crept into his psyche at times, he tried to put her out of his mind and find a local girlfriend. The first one he met at a Puerto Plata supermarket called La Serrana was named Irene. A young twenty-two, she had all the shapes in the right places and turned many male heads. But that relationship lasted less than three weeks. Mac felt a vibe from Irene, like she was just going through the motions of attraction but had another agenda. Although she performed dutifully in bed, at times her actions seemed devoid of passion. Oftentimes, immediately after sex, she would leave the room, go to Mac's computer, open up Facebook, a virtual gold mine for many Dominican women, and play for many hours.

And, of course, there were other things. Her mother was constantly getting sick, needing money for medication and the clinic. Mac didn't know if Irene had a Dominican boyfriend behind her, a chulo coercing her to extort money and profiting from it. But after a while he didn't care. The money requests just came in too fast and furious for his liking.

One night when Irene was over, after an hour of fun, she claimed she had received a text message from her mother, saying she needed her daughter at her side. Apparently, Mom needed a two-hundred peso pill that would cure all her health problems—a wonder drug. Irene asked for the money, promising to buy the life-saving medication, deliver it, and return promptly to Mac's side. Of course, she took the two hundred pesos and never returned that day. But, she returned two days later, needing more money for dear mother's illness. A thousand pesos, fifteen hundred pesos, and one time twenty-five hundred pesos. Many times Mac had acquiesced.

But one drunken night he got angry and sent some rather nasty text messages that spelled the end of their relationship: *All you want me for is my money. You're not interested in me at all. You're a liar. You don't love me one bit. You're like all the women in this area. All you do is prey on gringos for money. Why don't you fuck right off and find another sucker.* And that, she probably did, because it was the last time he ever heard from dear, sweet Irene.

Another girlfriend, Marie, had lasted two weeks. He had met the athletic-bodied twenty-four-year-old Haitian at a Costambar beach bar, slept with her that night, paid her, and sent her home. A few days later, sweet Marie showed up at his apartment, saying she had quit her job and wanted to be his live-in girlfriend. After all, she was hopelessly in love with him. For a time he believed her.

But there was a contradiction that eventually sent sweet Marie packing. Although she made love like a corpse, she claimed she loved him to death.

Boring. Not real. Bye-bye sweet Marie.

And there was a third, whom Mac still spoke to occasionally. Twenty-six-year-old Yannat was a bigger woman, not so much obese as large-boned and tall; but attractive enough with huge breasts. It had been those mammoth mammary glands that had caught Mac's drunken attention one night on the Malecon, whilst partying with the bros. So, he had promptly approached her, secured her phone number, and began a relationship. Of the three, Yannat's passion and love for him felt real. It didn't seem odd to him at the time that, after only two dates, she referred to him as her boyfriend. She was a great lover and gainfully employed as a waitress rather than a hooker, which was a rarity around these parts. She gave him little grief and even cooked and cleaned his apartment occasionally.

But there were a few things that formed barriers to a successful union. Some of Mac's friends didn't like what they called Yannet's snobbish attitude. Oftentimes, she would forget a common courtesy like a simple hello. When Mac reminded her of this social faux pas, she snapped: "I know! I'm an educated woman."

And then there were the niggling things that slowly made him aware they were not operating on the same intellectual plane. Yannet loved to watch cartoons and Spanish soap operas on television.

So, over time, boredom crept in and he began to give Yannat a wide berth; not returning calls and texts and avoiding the Malecon bar where she worked.

Too be sure, much of it was Mac's fault. He couldn't stop his drunken, womanizing ways and cheated on Yannet a few times. Even though over time he had become convinced his appetite for sex had nothing to do with any spell or curse; the temptation was just far too great to resist.

And he was not alone. Axel, Leonard and Sebastian had become his regular drinking buddies, good friends and brothers in sex adventures and foolery. The local ex-pats affectionately referred to them as the four stooges. From their escapades, many colorful, scary and funny stories were born. They added fuel to the gossip fire that was rife in the small beachfront community.

One such example: Leonard's ex-girlfriend showed up at his apartment one evening while he was having a few drinks with his girlfriend Stephanie. Even though Leonard hadn't spoken to Yaira in over a year, she arrived with two suitcases and promptly told Leonard she wanted to rekindle the romance and move in. Not knowing what to do, Leonard loaded Yaira, her luggage, and Stephanie into the car (Stephanie had remained calm and composed during the ordeal) and drove around Costambar. After a few minutes, Yaira said she was hungry so Leonard bought her a pizza. Not knowing what to do, he brought her to El Carey where his friends were.

After explaining the story to Mac, he asked, "Do you like her? Take her. She comes with luggage... and I'll throw in the pizza."

"Depends on the toppings. If it has olives or seafood on it, no way. But, if it's a Hawaiian... well maybe."

The joke was evidently missed on Leonard: "I don't know what the fuck toppings are on the fucking pizza."

Although he was hungry at the time, Mac respectfully and politely declined the offer. But, some other lonely gringo fool,

Billy Taggerty, wound up taking the Yaira all-inclusive package deal. A few days later, Billy was spotted running down the beach, pizza-less, being chased by a pleading, suitcase-toting Yaira. Apparently, Billy had found a stalker.

Sebastian had his own share of misadventures, many ending with him using his friend's apartments to sleep with multiple women while his loyal and faithful girlfriend Camila waited sometimes not so patiently at home. Occasionally, Camila got angry and locked him out of the apartment. Shouting and screaming ensued throughout the night. At times, the neighbors became angry and complained.

One night, the boys went out to the patio bar at Ocean World to celebrate Camila's birthday. While driving home certifiably pickled, Seb had the brilliant idea that an evening nude swim was in order. While the others waited in the car, he went to Cofresi beach, stripped, and went swimming. Leaving the ocean later, he was too drunk to remember where he had put his clothes. Dodging and hiding from resort security guards, he finally arrived at the vehicle and, naked, drove a car-full of drunken laughing fools home. At the Costambar gates, one guard grinned and winked at Seb, nearly sending Camila into a jealous tantrum. To this day, Seb still had nightmares about the guard's admiring ogles.

And another incident still gave him nightmares. On a drunken bet, Seb picked up a waitress in a bar, whose ass was the width of a pick-up truck, took her to a Cabana and had sex with her. He claimed when she sat in the hot tub she created a Tsunami wave so devastating the entire establishment had to be evacuated. It was a story he wouldn't live down any time soon; not if any of the other stooges had anything to say about it.

One night, they were bar-hopping in Sosua. Leonard felt someone grab him from behind, thought it was a robber, and instinctively spun around and delivered a hard, well-placed right to the jaw of an overly aggressive hooker. She dropped to the pavement like a sack of hammers and wound up costing Leonard a night in jail and two hundred dollars. Of course, it was Seb's cop connections that got him released.

Axel was found one morning by two security guards passed out on the beach, a naked hooker slumped over him. Luckily, because of his cop connections and military career—they admired and respected a soldier—gate police drove him home.

During one night of heavy drinking, Mac took some keys off a table he believed were his. Arriving at his apartment, he realized the keys would not open the door. Too drunk to do anything about it, he curled up outside the apartment and passed out. The next day, he learned Axel had passed out, outside his apartment, after realizing his keys also wouldn't unlock the door. They had stupidly taken one another's keys.

In February, during the Carnival, the stooges had partied hard on the Malecon. They got so drunk they became separated in the masses and went their separate ways. Mac wandered around aimlessly. A fight broke out and bottles flew. He ducked, ran, and narrowly avoided getting injured or killed. He learned later one person had been killed in the melee by a flying beer bottle to the head. Later that evening, Mac met three women, bought them drinks, and danced in the streets until all hours. After buying them pizza, he took the girls via taxi to a Cabana and, from at least what he could remember, had his way with all of them. He woke in a room penniless and alone, but with his cell phone intact. The usual debris littered the room.

The four stooges were becoming stoogier. Along with their womanizing, their blackouts were becoming more frequent. And blacker. Oftentimes, many hours were spent—the hungover morning after—trying to piece together the events of the night before; the bars they visited, what had happened to them and how they got home. They often repeated the same funny stories over and over without realizing people had heard them many times before.

With or without the malicious spirits, Mac had come full circle. At some point along the way—and who knew exactly when—his moral code and that of his brothers had become skewed. They thought it was okay to subjugate, exploit and objectify women, especially since many times the women encouraged it. With his near-insane lifestyle, the requisite follies and fuck ups were inevitable; at times the drunken anger was directed—or perhaps misdirected—at the Dominicans and their culture. And there were a few personal misunderstandings and arguments, but none severe enough as to have damaged the tight bond they had formed. Stuff like, "You fucked up last night... No, you did," or, "I paid that tab, it's your turn to buy," or, "That's my girl, keep your hands off." But Mac wondered when these petty arguments might erupt into something more violent, something that could put an irreparable rift in the brotherhood.

At times, he realized they were pushing the envelope and wondered when it would turn into a suicide mission. The stooges were burning out. If they continued down this dark path, somehow, somewhere, sometime, one or more of them was going to come to an untimely end. It had happened before to other such fools. It wouldn't be the first time—it wouldn't be the last.

At other times, Mac didn't care. As if in denial, he refused to think about it. Most times anyway. Occasionally, the words sex-addict and alcoholic would pop into his head, but he was reluctant to apply them to his condition. His new drunken lascivious lifestyle was too tempting, too hilarious, and too satisfying on many levels. And so, so much different from his lonely, unsatisfied, reclusive, depressing and loveless existence in PEI. *Loveless? What about Ophelia? Forget it.*

Wine, women and song. What could be better? I'm going to die anyway. I may as well go out with a smile on my face.

At that thought, he smiled. He had plans that April Fool's Day that promised to convert that smile into a satisfied grin. Sitting on his balcony that sunny morning—it was only eleven-thirty but, fuck, it was certainly noon somewhere in the world—he polished off his fourth Cuba libre, crushed out a smoke, forgot all about the drunken reflection and waved to Axel, who had just arrived at the locked gate below. "Hang on. I'll open it for you."

The four stooges had decided to celebrate April Fool's Day in fine fashion—with a pool party. They had decided that each one of them would call two of their most trusted hookers, tell them to bring a friend, and live it up. If everything worked out, they would have at least four girls for every guy—sixteen naked girls frolicking in the pool and four drunk and horny guys. What single (maybe even married) red-blooded man in his right mind would turn that down?

Right?

******

Two hours later the pool party was in full swing. Leonard and Axel were in the pool, splashing, laughing and playing with at least a half-dozen women in various stages of undress—some topless, others completely nude.

ACDC's Hell's Bells played on a radio:

I'm rolling thunder pouring rain
I'm coming on like a hurricane
My lightning's flashing across the sky
You're only young but you're gonna die
I won't take no prisoners won't spare no lives
Nobody's putting up a fight
I got my bell I'm gonna take you to hell
I'm gonna get ya satan get ya
Hells bells
Hells bells, you got me ringing
Hells bells, my temperature's high
Hells bells

Seb and Mac reclined poolside, a woman hanging off each arm.

They didn't get the turn-out they expected; only a dozen had arrived so far. But the night was young, the men eager, the booze plentiful, and the women playful. They had even anticipated the need for another suite. Since Mac's apartment was on the third floor and the complex didn't contain a poolside bathroom, they had rented a main-floor unit to serve three purposes: a fuck pad, a bar, and a bathroom. That way, the women wouldn't have to climb three sets of stairs to use the bathroom. That way, none of Mac's valuables would be at risk.

If Mac wanted to bring a woman up to his room, at least he would be there, mitigating the chance of theft.

They might have been in an alcoholic stupor, but they weren't stupid.

"This is the life, brother," Seb said, raising his drink.

Then he promptly snatched a handful of ice cubes from an ice bucket and dropped them down the bikini top of a woman in his arms. She screamed, jumped up, emptied the ice from her cleavage, and dove in the pool.

"You couldn't do this in Canada," Seb said.

"No," Mac said with a smile.

He lifted two cubes and moved them threateningly close the ample cleavage of a large-breasted woman nestled in alongside him.

"No you don't," the woman said, snatching the ice cubes from Mac's hand and stuffing them down his swim-shorts.

He removed them casually, threw them in the pool, and turned to Seb. "You're damned right you couldn't do this in Canada, hell North America for that matter. Even Hugh Hefner would be envious."

"Like I said," Seb said, turning to the woman on his left and casually cupping her breast. "We go back home, it's gonna be shock therapy."

"I actually think I'm going to get really depressed. I mean life is calm and peaceful there, but too damn calm and peaceful. And too many fucking laws. Regulated to death. Most of the outdoor restaurants, you can't even smoke. Can you imagine?"

"It's all about the balance, brother. It's all about balance. There you have too many laws, here not enough. There, the younger women won't even acknowledge you; here they're cock worshippers—all over you."

"Other than my work as a writer, and frankly I can do that anywhere in the world anyway, I don't know what the hell I'll do with myself when I return."

"When are you going back?"

"I was supposed to leave last week, but I changed it again. I leave May 6th."

"You still have time. And you can always change your ticket again. Maybe when you get there, you'll hop on a plane in another two weeks and come back."

"Maybe, you're right. I haven't given myself a lot of time to make friends there, but sometimes I don't know if I'll be able to cut it."

"Wouldn't surprise me. But, on the other hand, after all the shit you've been through, you might find it a refreshing change."

"I don't know. By the way, did I thank you for saving my life?"

"About six times."

"Okay... anyway, I was going to tell you a story—"

"Tell away."

"Before I left, before the nasty storms hit, I went to a few bars in a nearby small town. Some of the locals were looking at me like I'm a fucking alien from another planet, first of all. Second, the women were in a hen party. Talking together, barely paying attention to any of the other men, never mind me."

"In your country, you have to be more aggressive," Seb said. "I'm sure there are many opportunities there."

He circled the woman's nipple teasingly with an index finger. Her smile widened and she began gliding her hand along Seb's leg toward his crotch. Another woman climbed out of the pool with a splash. She sat on the other side of Seb, placing her hand on his other leg, and followed suit.

"Maybe, but that experience compared with the DR is night and fucking day," Mac said. "Granted, I wasn't in the best mood to be sociable, but I just wasn't feeling the love. At times I felt like a social misfit and I don't consider myself that. In any event, I had two beers and fucked off home, feeling a little unsatisfied and yes, maybe even a little depressed. I guess, as much as I criticize the DR, it's that lawlessness and adventure, the fact women give you the time of day—even the twenty-year-olds—that makes me want to return."

Seb peeled off the woman's bikini top and, cupping a well-formed breast in each hand, grinned and said: "Once you experience the good life, you don't want to go back... can't go back half the time, even if you wanted to..."

Although Seb was clearly getting aroused, his smile transformed into a slight frown. He removed his hands from the woman's breasts, gently lifted their hands off his legs, stood up and dove into the pool. He stuck his head out of the water just as Leonard, with two naked women, approached the appointed fuck pad. Seb wiped water from his face and shook his head. "It's not all that it's cracked up to be though... take us, we're a bunch of lost souls. Me, for example, fucking around like a loose cannon and I've got a good woman at home. I don't know how she puts up with my shit..."

"I believe you've said that before," Mac said.

"I did?"

"You did," Axel said, climbing out of the pool, two topless women trailing him. He turned to Leonard, who was just closing the door. "Give her one for me."

"Give her one for your fucking self," Leonard said, standing at the door with a wide grin. "And no cum in the pool. No pissing in the pool neither. I'm coming back for a swim."

He went inside and closed the door.

"Hope you can get it up, old man," Seb said. He climbed out of the pool, grabbed a towel and began drying himself. "I'm getting downright philosophical for April Fool's Day. This is supposed to be a pool party."

"The joke's on you," Axel said, sitting down with a drink. "Somber on April Fool's Day."

"Well, I'm going to change that," Seb said, extending a hand to each of his female companions. A woman on each arm, he turned to Mac. "Hey, brother, mind if I use your room for a bit? Don't worry, I'll keep an eye on your computer and shit. And I trust Lisa and Jenny anyway. Been with them before. They're cool."

Mac nodded, tossing his keys to Seb. "No problem... no shot-spots on the sheets."

Seb escorted Lisa and Jenny to the foot of the stairs and glanced back. "How about on your toothbrush?"

"Fuck you."

They disappeared.

"Cheers, bro," Axel said, holding up his cup.

"Cheers to you, bro," Mac said, taking a swallow. "To the best pool party ever."

"Not like the last one," Axel said. "I sure as fuck hope not anyway."

Some of the women formed a hen party of their own, for the moment leaving Mac and Axel to talk. It didn't matter. They knew soon enough their time was coming. Mac also knew, in all likelihood, the party would go well into the wee hours of the morning and they would probably end up fucking in the pool, on the patio, and anywhere else their horny little hearts or dicks desired.

"You know I saw Livia last night?" Axel said.

"You remember?"

"Yeah, I wasn't that pissed for a change."

Mac had been brought up to date on Axel's romance with Livia. What he had neglected to tell Axel—he didn't think it mattered anymore anyway—was that he once had a relationship with her. One that had ended rather poorly.

"How did it go?"

"I don't know. She told me she had a relationship with you once and fucked it all up. I didn't know that, Mac, I swear, otherwise I wouldn't have even gone near her."

"It doesn't matter. I didn't even remember her when I first saw her here I was so fucked up. Never mind that, I didn't remember her the second time neither, nor the third, nor the fourth... it took her coming up to the hospital, admitting who she was and apologizing before I remembered her. Forget about it. If you're able to have a good relationship with her, you have my blessing."

"Thanks. Cheers. That means a lot to me."

"So, getting back to my original question, how did it go?"

"I don't know... I'm far from perfect; so is she, but I think I love her and she loves me."

"If that's what you want, maybe you have a chance."

"Are you kidding me, bro? Are you serious? Fuck sakes, look at us, man. Look at these women... look at all this booze. This is what we like. This is what we do. This is us, brother, this is who we are!"

Mac was getting too drunk to play devil's advocate, if that was the right term. And besides, the woman on his right was starting to peel her bikini top off. His attention was diverted as she unhinged her voluptuous melons and pushed them into his face, smothering him with flesh. With a mouthful of melons, he was hard-pressed to reply even if he wanted to. But, tasting the sweet and succulent fruit of his desire, he had to admit the party had a slightly seedy and sour edge to it.

Axel's negativity, or was he just being a realist?

Seb's so-called soul-searching.

Even Leonard had seemed more caustic than usual, and Mac felt himself unable to completely relax. It was as if there was some tacit realization—almost a palpable fear—that they had gone too far with their misadventures, pushed too hard, and now teetered on the edge of some dangerous precipice.

But in spite of the uncomfortable vibe, the pool party went on and went wild well into the night. They all got fucked and sucked multiple times in multiple locations and positions (yes, there was cum in the pool) with multiple partners. The brothers put aside their reservations, became drunkenly jolly together as they had done so often, and enjoyed themselves.

For a time.

At about two-thirty in the morning, a sliding glass door from a second-floor balcony opened and an angry, elderly French-Canadian man stormed out, shaking his fist. "I told you nicely before" (which none of them remembered, but that didn't mean it didn't happen). Now, I'm going to tell you not so nicely. Keep the goddamned noise down and take your party inside or I'm going to call the landlord. You can't do this in public, naked women everywhere, making all this noise to all hours. Who do you think you are? Don't you have any respect?"

Axel wasn't in any position to have any respect for the soliloquy, although it was delivered with some eloquence. He was passed out on a lawn chair, snoring loudly, with two topless women nestled alongside him.

And Seb, at that hour, didn't have respect for much, least of all an angry man disturbing his right to party, frolic in the pool and fornicate at will. He began arguing with the man in Spanish, although Mac, who had helped out Jean with some translation previously, knew Jean didn't speak or understand Spanish. But that didn't stop Seb. He said he had as much right here as they did and well, Jean could just "go fuck yourself if you don't like it."

Mac told Seb that perhaps they should take the party inside.

Leonard also urged Seb to "shut the fuck up, please. They're his neighbors and he has to live with them."

Maybe Jean did understand after all, or maybe it was Seb's tone. But, he quickly retreated inside his apartment and slid the sliding-glass door closed.

Finally, Jean got his desired outcome. The brothers, or stooges, ushered most of the women out. Leonard brought one with him into the main-floor suite, and Seb followed, leading two of his own.

Mac, for his part, woke Axel up. With Jenny and Lisa in tow, they staggered up to Mac's apartment to have a nightcap, a little more sex perhaps, if they could still get it up, and then time for beddy-bye. Good night, Jenny. Good night, Lisa. Good night, Leonard. Good night, Seb. Good night, Axel. Good night, Dick. Good night, John Boy. All tucked in and sleeping peacefully. Another night in paradise in the erotic and exotic Caribbean.

And that's how it all ended.

Almost.

Mac brought Jenny into the bedroom and left Lisa and Axel to their own devices in the living room. It wasn't long before he heard them snoring. But, far from tired, Mac felt a little frisky. Rum sometimes did that to him. And, to his good luck and good fortune, so did Jenny. And hot damn, was that woman a passionate lover. She kissed, caressed, stroked and sucked him, finally mounting him in the cowgirl position, pumping him long and hard before they climaxed together in an intensely powerful, shuddering, moaning and screaming (at least on Jenny's part) and mutually satisfying orgasm.

Wow, what a night! What an orgasm! That pleasant thought in mind, Mac finally drifted off to sleep.

But, five minutes later, his sleep was disrupted by the deafening sound of a gunshot, then shattering glass, then shards of glass flying everywhere—dangerously close to his head. Mac got up and stared in horror at the bloodied woman who stepped through what remained of the sliding-glass door and into his bedroom.

It was Violeta.

But there was something very different about her. She was carrying a pistol in one hand and wielding a large knife in the other. Her eyes glowed a bright fiery red, much different from the way Mac remembered them. There was madness and rage in those eyes.

She burst through the jagged edges of glass and didn't waste any time. As Jenny woke up abruptly, Violeta trained the pistol at her head and fired twice, one bullet smashing through her eye, the other tearing into her throat. Jenny spat a mouthful of blood that dribbled down her chin. Her head sank into the pillow and she fell into a permanent sleep.

"No, no," Mac shouted, charging at Violeta.

She sidestepped and he smashed into the wall. As he turned around, gripping the wall frantically to avoid falling down, she fired again. The bullet missed him narrowly, caught the wall at an angle, and ricocheted around the room.

"You dare to fuck with the spirits," Violeta said in a raspy, angry voice that was clearly not her own. "Now, you pay."

She tucked the knife into her black shorts, levelled the weapon and took aim. Mac leaped forward and, with his right hand, grabbed her wrist, pushing it upward as she pulled the trigger. The gun blasted towards the ceiling, hit the rotating ceiling fan and zinged out the smashed sliding-glass door and into a black sky lit by a glowing white full moon.

Neighborhood dogs started barking.

A struggle ensued, Mac gripping Violeta's wrists with both hands. She struggled to free them. They were both locked in an embrace of death, dancing around the bedroom under the spasmodically gyrating ceiling fan.

Mac couldn't believe the woman's supernatural strength and he knew he wouldn't be able to keep up this dance of death for much longer; although he had become remarkably sober remarkably fast. A thought occurred to him: *Wake up Axel, he's military, he'll know what to do.*

Violeta grimaced, twisted her body and flung Mac into the wall. He felt sharp pain as his head struck it and his world began to grow black. He slid down the wall and wilted onto the ceramic tiles, willing himself to get up, at least roll over before it was too late. But, too concussed from the blow, his body would not obey foggy brain commands.

She approached and stood over him. She pointed the gun at his head.

"Axel," Mac shouted. "I need your fucking help. PLEASE!"

As a gray-black fog closed in around Mac, he reached out, grabbed a pillow that had fallen on the floor and put it over his head. If he was to die, he didn't want to see the pure evil in the eyes of his malicious executioner. He covered his head with the pillow, and tried to summon the image of Ophelia. Miraculously, her beautiful face emerged in his mind's eye. Her penetrating eyes bored into his.

She frowned and said, "Do not fear death."

Then a smile slowly crept across her lips and her image suddenly vanished.

"Ophelia," Mac shouted. "Save me... PLEASE!"

Violeta plugged three bullets into the pillow and Mac's foggy gray world faded to black.

******

Axel burst through the door. "No," he shouted, charging at Violeta and smashing her into the wall. They struggled in a macabre dance of death for a few seconds.

Then Violeta picked Axel up by the throat and, like a ragdoll, tossed him out the open bedroom door. He crashed onto the hallway floor, slid along it, and smashed into the kitchen island, instinctively curling up.

Axel felt blood oozing from a cut on his forehead. His world grew black.

Lisa screamed and ran from the room, leaving the apartment door ajar.

Violeta walked purposefully into the kitchen, stood above Axel, and lowered the gun to his head. He swept an arm across the floor and took out her feet. She flew into the air and crashed hard on her ass.

Still holding the gun, she rolled over and mounted Axel.

"You dare interfere with the power of Kalfu," she said, pointing the gun at his head. "Now you die."

"You fuck off and die, bitch," Axel said, grabbing her wrist at the last second and changing the trajectory of the bullet. It smashed through a window, shattering shards of glass that flew onto the balcony, the pool and the patio below.

Somehow, Axel managed to struggle free and get up. Violeta leaped to her feet, tucked the piece in her shorts, grabbed him by the neck with both hands and began strangling him to death. Axel pounded on her arms but was unable to release her death grip. He felt his eyes bulging in their sockets and gasped for breath. His face turned bright pink, then dark red, then puce purple. With rapidly draining strength, he punched Violeta in the mouth. The blow snapped her head back momentarily and he saw, with dying satisfaction, blood trickling down her lip.

She's human after all. She bleeds. And that was the last thought he had.

Suddenly a powerful force lifted the locked combatants. They hovered, suspended in mid-air momentarily, and then were thrust swiftly out the broken living room window and into the night.

Chapter Twenty-Seven

The night was dark and calm. Overhead, the full moon shone brightly and the stars twinkled brilliantly. A small fire blazed in a forested area of La Reina, a little village a few miles from the Haitian border. It was the same village where Mac was taken after he had been kidnapped and almost sacrificed to angry Voodoo spirits. Around the fire sat intent faces. They quietly watched a man sitting cross-legged in a nearby circle, head bowed. He was bare-chested, bare-legged, naked but for a pair of black shorts.

As he sat quietly, eyes staring into the dirt, Mac realized he was actually doing three things: meditating, invoking the powerful spirit of love, and reflecting on what was then and what was now. Then, he was a lost soul with no power of communion with the spirit world.

Now, since Magdeline Ortega, the newly appointed spirit of love, had come to him in a vision one night, he was on an apprenticeship to become a houngan, a Voodoo priest. In the powerful vision, Maggie said Bondye, the Supreme God, had granted her wish to become a spirit. He was angry at Kalfu and the Baron Samedi not only for overstepping their boundaries, but fighting amongst themselves and disrupting the natural order of things. For their crimes, Bondye had sentenced them to three months of hellish suffering in the dark and cavernous realm of the underworld.

It had been Maggie who had saved Mac's life. Violeta, possessed by Kalfu at the time, had missed with all three bullets when she had shot into the pillow. And it had been Maggie's intervention, possessing the little girl Katrina that had also played a monumental part in Mac's survival. Maggie, as it turned out, had made it part of her life's mission to redeem Mac from his debaucherous ways.

But she wanted something in return.

Fractus Menses, practicing on the evil side of Voodoo, had destroyed the moral of the La Reina villagers and converted many of them to evil. Promising to mentor him every step of the way, Maggie wanted Mac to live in La Reina as a Voodoo priest and right the moral path of the corrupted villagers. And she wanted him to adopt little Katrina, who, after a forest fire destroyed her house and killed her parents, was left homeless and without anyone to care for her. Katrina had also survived the macabre Voodoo ceremony and Maggie had cured her of her madness. But even her extended family had been killed in the inferno that had gutted a small section of the village.

So Mac, who knew for a long time he was on a suicide mission—*three strikes, yer out, my friend*—accepted. What did he have to lose? Better to live on the edge—maximum risk, maximum reward—than to rot away on some paradise-like beachfront property in PEI with a self-serving agenda geared only to his own happiness and well-being. Mac had changed his plane ticket again. He was now scheduled to fly out May 31st, but he knew it would only be to clean up a few business items, slap a *FOR SALE* sign on the property, and return to his calling. By helping others, maybe he could save himself. Besides, it would give him an opportunity to be close to his friends in Costambar.

Mac thought they needed him now more than ever. *For better or worse, these misfits are my family, my brothers.* Sure they were lost souls, maybe alcoholics and sex addicts, but they were loyal. They watched his ass and were there for him when he needed them. Loyalty is hard to find. If you find it, keep it.

And Mac hoped one day to help his friends find a happier and more peaceful existence, perhaps free from all the licentiousness and booze. That, of course, would come in time, when some of them returned.

After the attempt on his life, once again, it had been Seb, with his cop connections, and five hundred dollars that had gotten Mac out of trouble. But, soon afterward, Seb had returned home to Switzerland, claiming he was "on a meditative journey of to find myself."

Leonard, for his part, also disappeared. His girlfriend Stephanie returned to hooking full-time, leaving him devastated. He returned to Canada because "this fucking country is starting to get to me and I need a break from it before I burn out."

And then there was Axel. As if on cue, he emerged from a small hut holding a half-full bottle of rum and grinning. Livia followed. They joined hands, walked to the fire, and sat down quietly beside Mac. They didn't want to disturb Mac's deep reverie and invocation ceremony. Everything was on the line for them. They wanted to change their ways and wanted Mac's connection with the spirit of love to bond them healthily, happily, and forever in love. Axel had decided he owed Maggie that much after she had saved his life. When he and Violeta were violently thrust from the apartment window, Maggie had magically separated them. Axel landed in the pool and survived relatively uninjured while Violeta splattered on the concrete below and was killed on impact, her mangled, blood-soaked face unrecognizable to police.

Slowly and softly, the drums began to beat.

Mac looked to the couple. "Are you ready?"

They nodded.

As Mac reflected, it was not missed on him how special this ceremony was. It was April 16th, the week of Semana Santa, a time when many locals celebrated the resurrection of Jesus Christ and their most important holiday. Ironically, during many of those celebrations, when the drunken mobs swarmed the beaches to celebrate, people got killed: flying bottles, vehicular collisions, alcohol-induced violence and rage.

But Mac wasn't thinking of death. No, he was thinking of rebirth; his rebirth, the rebirth of his friends and congregation and that special someone. He raised his head, looked at Axel, and nodded.

Axel took a large swallow from the rum bottle and passed it to Livia, who did the same and passed it to Mac. Mac drank, placed it between his legs, and nodded to the drummers, who quickened the drum beat. He raised a hand and six female followers stood, looked up into the dark heavens, and began chanting while slowly dancing around the blaze.

He nodded to a man kneeling at a thatched-roof hut. The man opened a makeshift door.

Ophelia stepped out and eyed Mac affectionately. Taking her hand, the man led her to Mac. She sat down beside him, kissed him passionately on the lips, took his hand, and began watching the ritualistic dancers.

A small murmur rolled through the seated congregants. And then they were silent.

After nearly dying, Mac had in a sober moment phoned Ophelia and poured his heart out to her, telling her almost everything that had happened to him. "I love you and need you. I realize that now." To his surprise, she boarded a plane two days later and met him in Costambar.

"You actually got me on your last call," she said after arriving. "And that was a drunk-dial call. Maybe there is something to be said for drunk-dialing."

Ophelia might not have believed all the Voodoo stuff. But, she had been with Mac when he saw the vision of Maggie, the spirit of love. And she had seen it too. Maggie had entreated Ophelia to join Mac and assured her that Mac's love for her was real.

"I'm glad you came," Mac said, lighting a cigar and taking two deep drags. He blew three perfect smoke rings into the air and they slowly disappeared. "I need you so much."

Ophelia laughed. "You had me at drunk-dialing."

"I love you," Mac said, passing her the bottle, an integral part of the ceremony.

Ophelia took a drink, wiped a small rivulet of rum from her chin, and smiled. "I love you too." She passed the bottle back to Mac.

He returned it to its natural resting place between his legs.

Katrina ran up, gave both her adopted mother and father a big kiss on the cheek, and sat down cheerfully in Ophelia's lap. Ophelia wrapped her arms around the little girl. "Watch honey. Daddy's going to save some people."

Livia and Axel gazed lovingly in into one another's eyes.

A lone tear rolled down Mac's cheek.

The drumbeat intensified.

The chanting grew louder.

The movement of the dancers became frenetic, frenzied almost.

A dagger-wielding man led a squealing goat into the circle. Another man joined him and they restrained the struggling beast. After the ceremony, there would be a feast and a wild party that would go on well into the night.

After a few minutes, Mac opened his arms to the heavens and spoke. "I entreat you, almighty Maggie, spirit of love, bring Axel and Livia, me and Ophelia, together in a powerful bond of loyalty, respect, trust, honesty and love. Let us not stray from the path of fidelity for we might love, cherish, honor and obey each other in sickness and in health—until death do us part."

The End

Also by William Blackwell

Phantom Rage, Poison Rage, Infected Rage
Nightmare's Edge
Resurrection Point
Brainstorm
Rule 14
Assaulted Souls
Assaulted Souls II
Assaulted Souls III
Blood Curse
Black Dawn
The Strap
The End is Nigh
Orgon Conclusion
Freaky Franky
The Witch's Tombstone
The Dark Menace
Tales of Damnation
In Your Dreams
Macabre Alley
A Head for an Eye

In Your Dreams Preview

"On the surface, it's a gripping horror thriller with brutal, shocking twists. But beneath that, it's a thought-provoking exploration of obsession, loneliness, and the terrifying power our subconscious holds over us. The writing is bold, cinematic, and immersive—it reminded me of a cross between Clive Barker and early Stephen King, yet with a unique, modern edge." -Amazon

Alienated from humanity, Oliver Gimble is a self-indulgent sloth who finds vicarious comfort in binge-watching horror movies and gorging on junk food. During sleep, he escapes into a meticulously constructed dream world where he discovers carnal delight with an enigmatic woman called Stella.

His bizarre lifestyle begins to unravel when he meets Carmen Weathersby, a lonely woman, who in Oliver's mind's eye mysteriously transforms into Stella, the woman of his dreams. But soon Oliver realizes Stella is actually interfering with his new relationship and will go to any lengths, even murder, to possess him.

When Carmen's elderly mother suffers a heart attack, fingers point to Stella.

Suddenly, people close to Carmen start dying—brutally and inexplicably.

Careening helplessly down into a cryptic and otherworldly realm somewhere between reality and perception, Carmen and Oliver struggle to try and solve the macabre mystery before it's too late.

A multi-layered, horrifying journey of self-discovery, *In Your Dreams* examines the powerful and shocking connections between our conscious and subconscious worlds—boldly questioning the very nature of reality.

About the Author

Canadian dark fiction author William Blackwell studied journalism at Mount Royal University and English literature at The University of British Columbia. He worked as a journalist and a newspaper editor for many years before pursuing his passion for storytelling. His novels have been characterized as graphic, edgy, and at times terrifying. Currently living on a secluded acreage on Prince Edward Island, Blackwell finds much of his inspiration from Mother Nature, odd people, traveling, and bizarre nightmares.

Author Comments

Thank you for reading this book. I would be eternally grateful if you would post a book review on your favorite book retailer website. A positive review is the highest compliment a writer can receive. Reviews are crucial to the success of any author and they help readers discover new books. You don't have to say much. A few sentences will suffice.

In other news, I have a gift for you. Complete the signup form below with your name and email address and download a FREE copy of *Resurrection Point*, a dark tale about the horrifying consequences of experimenting with death and resurrection. You're only agreeing to be kept up to date on blog posts, new releases, and freebies. I promise I won't spam you and you can unsubscribe at any time.

Thanks again for your support.

http://www.wblackwell.com/free-ebook/